"Just stay away from me!"

"I can hardly do that if we're going to renew our marriage vows," Kyle said. "I'm not cut out for celibacy.... What you need—"

"What I need is for *you* to take off the way you came!" Shannon flung at him.

"I said there were *reasons* why we should get back together," he responded.

She eyed him warily, still not convinced that he wasn't planning on making another grab. "There's no possible reason you could find that would matter enough, I can tell you that now!"

"Not even if it means my sister's daughter spending the rest of her childhood in an orphanage?"

KAY THORPE was born in Sheffield, England, in 1935. She tried out a variety of jobs after leaving school. Writing began as a hobby, becoming a part of her life only after she had her first completed novel accepted for publication in 1968. Since then, she's written over sixty books and now lives with her husband, son, German shepherd dog and lucky black cat on the outskirts of Chesterfield in Derbyshire. Her interests include reading, hiking and travel.

Kay Thorpe
CONTRACT WIFE

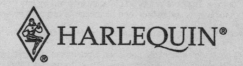

HARLEQUIN®

TORONTO • NEW YORK • LONDON
AMSTERDAM • PARIS • SYDNEY • HAMBURG
STOCKHOLM • ATHENS • TOKYO • MILAN • MADRID
PRAGUE • WARSAW • BUDAPEST • AUCKLAND

ISBN 0-373-18731-9

CONTRACT WIFE

First North American Publication 2000.

Copyright © 1998 by Kay Thorpe.

Visit us at www.eHarlequin.com

Printed in U.S.A.

CHAPTER ONE

THERE it came again! Sitting bolt upright in bed, hair standing metaphorically if not quite literally on end, Shannon strained her ears to pick up further sounds. That something was moving about downstairs was certain; whether human or animal was the question.

The sensible thing might be to stay where she was, but if it did turn out to be a burglar it was surely better to try scaring him off while he *was* still downstairs by making some noise of her own.

Anyway, came the fleeting thought as she slid from the bed, since when had she done the sensible thing?

The boiler must have gone out, she realised, feeling the chill strike through as she crept barefoot along the narrow landing. If something was going to go wrong with the heating, you could bet it would do it on one of the coldest nights of the year!

Leaning incautiously over the somewhat rickety bannister, she could see the flicker of torchlight coming from the kitchen—hear the unmistakable sound of a drawer being opened and closed, followed by a muffled curse. Definitely human, and definitely male; neither classification of any comfort. A shout might suffice to shift him—though it might well shift him in the wrong direction if he realised she was a woman on her own.

The stick used to lift the loft trapdoor was leaning against the wall. It wasn't much of a weapon, but better than nothing if she needed to defend herself. The self-defence classes she'd attended last year had been geared towards close combat, and whilst she could appreciate the probable incapacitating effect of a well-aimed knee to the groin, or the edge of a hand to the throat, she'd just as soon not have to put either technique to the test.

Lifting the stick, she banged it down hard on the rail, at the same time yelling, 'Craig, there's someone downstairs!'

There was a sudden loud crack as the section of bannister she was leaning against gave way, propelling her forward to swing like a monkey from the still semi-attached spar, the stick clattering to the hall floor below. It wasn't a long way to fall, but, with only a rug to fall on, a mite too far for Shannon to contemplate letting go her hold immediately—although judging from the creaking sounds it wasn't going to be long before she had no choice.

Everything else momentarily driven from her mind by the shock, she tensed even further when two hands seized her above the ankles, kicking out frenziedly in an effort to dislodge the firm grasp.

'Get off!' she yelled. 'Just get off!'

'You'd rather I let you fall?' asked an all-too familiar voice, rendering an even greater shock. 'Relax, will you, or you'll bring the lot down? Let go, and I'll catch you.'

As choices went, she was caught between the devil and the deep blue sea, but, as Kyle had pointed out, her support wasn't going to last much longer. Drawing a hard breath, she did as he had instructed and released her hold, eyes squeezed shut as she dropped into strong arms.

Her rescuer made no attempt to set her on her feet, holding her without strain. Shannon could feel the prickle of wool against the bare arm pressed close to his chest, and through it the steady beat of his heart. Her own was thudding like a triphammer, and not wholly because of the fall. It had been a long time since she'd known the feel of these arms about her.

'Put me down!' she ordered, shutting out the memories with fierce intent. 'What the devil are you doing here anyway?'

'Looking for you, what else?' he said. 'Good thing too, considering the Tarzan act.'

'Which wouldn't have happened if you hadn't broken in,' she pointed out. 'And will you please put me down?'

He did so unceremoniously, rocking her on her heels. In this light—or lack of it, to be more precise—the grey eyes looked almost black, but there was no disguising the angles and planes of those hard-boned, handsome features, the firm lines of the mouth that had driven her so wild with desire in the past. The thick white sweater made his shoulders look broader than ever, her lack of footwear affording him a good seven or eight inches' advantage in height. Altogether a dangerous combination.

'For the record, I didn't break in,' he said. 'I didn't have to. You'd left the back door unlocked.' There was a short pause, a change of tone. 'Seems your Craig is a pretty heavy sleeper!'

Too confused to remember her ploy for a moment, Shannon gaped at him. 'How did you know about—?' She broke off abruptly as her mind cleared, biting her lip. 'There's no one else here,' she admitted. 'I was just making out there was a man in the house.'

His lips slanted. 'There *is* a man in the house. A very cold, very hungry one, I might add. I'd have been here hours ago if I hadn't had to dig myself out more than once.'

Shannon's brows drew together. 'Dig yourself out from what?'

'The snow, of course. It's drifting feet deep in parts.'

The frown deepened. 'It was only an inch or so when I went to bed.'

'Which was when?'

'Around eleven, I suppose.'

'It's gone four now, and, like I said, it's drifting. I'm lucky to have found the place at all. It's way off the beaten track!'

'The very reason my aunt bought the cottage. She likes to get away from it all.'

Adrenalin no longer pumping through her bloodstream the way it had been, Shannon gave a sudden shiver as the chill started to get to her, for the first time becoming conscious that she was wearing nothing but a thin silk nightdress. That Kyle would have been very much aware of it too when he'd held her she didn't doubt. Pressing though they were, the whys and wherefores of this bolt from the blue would have to wait until she got some clothes on. Her teeth were going to start chattering any minute.

'If you're staying up, you'd better go and get dressed,' Kyle reinforced. 'Just tell me where the spare fuses might be first. Looking for them by torchlight is no easy task.'

'You mean the electricity's off?' she said, and could have bitten off her tongue, sensing the derisive expression in the grey eyes.

'The main fuse has blown. Luckily it's the household one, not the supply—although it won't make any difference if there's no spare cartridge. In that case, it will be out to the woodshed for some logs, and a hope that the sitting-room chimney was swept recently.'

Shannon doubted it. Her aunt wasn't the kind to give much thought to such practicalities, and it was unlikely that the farmer's wife who generally kept an eye on the place would have had it done. No point in worrying about it now, anyway. If the fireplace had to be used, it had to be used, soot or no soot.

'Try the cabinet beside the sink,' she said, with vague memories of having seen fuse wire and such. She was shivering for real now. 'Second drawer down, I think.'

'Let's hope you're right.' He was turning as he spoke, switching on the torch he had picked up again from somewhere. 'See you in a minute or two, all being well. And watch yourself on the landing,' he added over a shoulder.

From which vantage point would you advise? Shannon almost retorted, but sarcasm had never proved a very effective weapon where her husband was concerned. Leaving aside the question of how he had known where she was, what could possibly be so important that he had to follow her out here? she wondered, heading back upstairs. In the eighteen months since they'd separated there had been little contact of any kind.

Perhaps he'd decided it was time to talk about getting a divorce. Having once made a decision, Kyle acted on it regardless. Well, fine by her, she told herself hardily, ignoring the deep-down pang. It might even help her make up her mind about Craig.

Back in the bedroom, she pulled warm leggings up over slim hips, and slid her arms into a thick navy blue sweater. The fleecy-lined leather boots weren't intended for house wear, but even if Kyle could sort out the electricity it was going to take time to warm the place through again, and her toes already felt like blocks of ice.

He hadn't been exaggerating about the weather, she confirmed, looking out of the window on a white world. Judging from the amount of snow still clinging to the bodywork of the Range Rover parked up in front of the garage, he hadn't been exaggerating about the digging out either. His own fault anyway. He should have turned back when he realised conditions were deteriorating. Being born intractable was no excuse.

She must have left the dressing-table lamp on when she went to bed because it suddenly came to life again, along with the welcome hum of the central-heating pump. Semi-reflective now, the window glass showed a vivacious, somewhat wilful face with its stubborn little chin and generously curved mouth, the wide-set green eyes slightly tilted at the corners. Cat's eyes, Kyle had called them. If she had paid heed to her feline senses on first meeting him, came the wry thought now, she might have been spared a whole lot of subsequent heartache.

Turning away from the window, she seized a clip from the dressing table and fastened the heavy fall of corn-gold hair back into her nape, feeling the chill still striking through her. A hot drink was what was needed. That, and a good dose of backbone.

The smell of frying bacon wafted up the stairs to meet her as she descended. Kyle had obviously wasted no time in looking through her stores. Early though it was, she felt the stirring of hunger. Weekday breakfasts usually consisted of cereals followed by a slice of toast and coffee, but, faced with that smell, she was ready to make an exception for once.

'I hope you're doing enough of that for two,' she said, donning nonchalance like a cloak as she entered the country-style kitchen with its cheerful yellow and white decor and warm pine units. 'If I have to be up at this unearthly hour I may as well go the whole hog!'

'Plenty for all,' Kyle assured her. 'One egg or two?'

'One will be ample, thanks.'

Shannon took a seat at the small central table, watching the expert way in which he broke the eggs one-handed against the side of the pan. Had she attempted to do that they would have finished up anywhere but in the pan!

If he hadn't taken up writing for a living, he could probably have made just as big a mark as a chef. A man of many talents was her husband. It was basic integrity that was missing.

What definitely and disturbingly wasn't missing was the effect he had on her senses. He was so wonderfully built: shoulders broad, hips lean, thighs hard with muscle. She tremored deep down inside at the memory of that same muscular hardness possessing her; of the feel of his hands on her body, the long, tensile fingers so exquisitely knowledgeable. However much she might think of Craig as a person, he didn't arouse the same degree of need in her; that much she had to acknowledge.

'How's Paula?' she asked, maintaining the insouciant note.

'No idea,' Kyle returned equably, flipping over the eggs without breaking the yokes, the way she liked them herself.

Registering the sudden lurch of her heart, Shannon fought to control her treacherous emotions. 'Loss of interest on whose part?' she managed with creditable dispassion.

'Mutual agreement.' He transferred the eggs to the waiting plates, where the bacon and tomatoes already resided, then turned off the burner and brought both plates across to the table, which was ready laid. 'Tuck in while it's good and hot. There's coffee in the pot.'

'Efficient as ever,' she commented as he took his seat opposite, unable this time to keep the brittleness wholly at bay. 'Electrician, cook, author supreme—is there *anything* you're not good at?'

The ironic lift of his eyebrow brought warmth to her

cheeks and further tension to her stomach muscles. She had left herself wide open to that, she thought ruefully.

'I'm obviously not so hot when it comes to relation-ships,' he said. 'I just can't seem to keep my women.'

'Probably because the last thing you really want is commitment,' Shannon clipped back. 'You married me because, unlike my forerunners, I wouldn't let you have me any other way, but it didn't take long for the novelty to wear off!'

The grey eyes revealed no particular emotion. 'It would have been a whole lot longer if you hadn't thrown in the towel.'

'I threw in the towel, as you so cornily put it, because I wasn't willing to share you with another woman! Or should I say other *women*?' Shannon was too incensed by the accusation to maintain her outer composure, eyes flashing green fire, nails digging into her palms as she fought the almost overwhelming desire to smash her hand across the lean, hard cheek. 'What did you expect? A pat on the back and a "well done"?'

Just for a moment there was an answering spark in the grey eyes, a tensing of muscle about the jawline be-neath the morning stubble, then his face relaxed again, his shoulders lifting in a brief shrug. 'All water under the bridge, isn't it?'

He'd used *that* cliché with deliberation, Shannon knew. A dig at her, who had perhaps used such phrasing a mite too often in her working life. Not that she gave a damn. Success was success, whichever genre one chose to work in.

'You're right,' she said, taking a hold on herself along with the knife and fork. 'There's no point in raking over dead coals.'

Hungry as she had felt a few minutes ago, she had to force the food down. Kyle ate with enjoyment, obviously little affected by the brief altercation. But when had she ever been able to get under his skin for long? When had he ever shown any real depth of emotion? He had married her because his male ego wouldn't allow him any other course, not for love. He wouldn't know love if it hit him in the face!

They had finished eating and were onto coffee before she felt sufficiently in command of herself to start the ball rolling again.

'How did you know where I was?' she asked.

'I rang your mother when I couldn't reach you in town,' he returned. 'She gave me directions.'

Probably in the hope of a reconciliation, Shannon reflected. Her mother had always thought a lot of Kyle, to the point of refusing to take sides over the break-up.

'You could have phoned,' she pointed out.

The grey eyes held steady. 'This wasn't something to be discussed over the phone.'

She said flatly, 'You mean you want to talk about a divorce?'

Kyle studied her in silence for a moment before answering, expression hard to read. 'What makes you think I might want a divorce?'

'Now that Paula's gone from your life, you mean?' Shannon gave a brief shrug, pretending an indifference she was still a long way from feeling. 'I doubt if you've been celibate since. Anyway, I can't think of any other reason you might have for following me here.'

'The question I keep asking myself is why you're here at all,' he said. 'You're not writing at the moment, so it's hardly a case of needing some peace and quiet.'

'How do you know I'm not writing?' she prevaricated, unwilling to admit her reasons for wanting to get away on her own for a spell.

'I asked your editor. She said you were taking a break.'

'So I am. A winter break. The cottage is as good a place as any for a little R and R.'

'In summer, maybe. Right now, I'd say your apartment was a better place to be.'

'Flat,' she corrected with purpose. 'It's rather less ritzy than your place—assuming you still have it?'

Kyle slanted a lip. 'I still have it. The house too. But you'd know that, of course. I could hardly get rid of it without your agreement—even if I wanted to.'

'You're entitled to do whatever you like with the house,' Shannon responded smartly. 'It was your money that paid for it. I already made it clear I want nothing from you, Kyle—in any shape or form.'

The slant increased. 'If you're trying to provoke me, you're going the right way about it.'

She widened her eyes at him with deliberation. 'Heaven forbid!'

'Stop acting like one of your heroines,' he retorted cuttingly. 'Unless you're after having me act like one of your heroes, maybe?'

'Considering you've never read any of my books, you wouldn't have any idea how my heroes are likely to act!' she shot back, and saw his mouth stretch into a taunting smile.

'I've read enough to have a good idea. One thing they're not is wimpish, I'll grant you. But then, you'd never have fallen for me in the first place if it was yes-men you liked.'

True enough, Shannon had to admit. He was the only man she had ever come across who came anywhere close to the kind of men she wrote about. The difference being that she had control over her characters, while Kyle was a law unto himself. Which hardly made provocation of any kind a good idea.

'There's such a thing as moderation,' she responded, trying for a modicum of the same. 'Such a thing as fidelity too. You obviously thought you could have all the advantages of marriage without having your bachelor instincts curtailed in any way.'

Leaning back now in his chair, feet stretched, hands clasped comfortably behind his head—devastating with or without stubble on his jaw—Kyle regarded her without a trace of guilt or discomfiture. 'We've been through all that too many times. I've no intention of going through it all again. If we start over, we do it from here.'

'Start over!' Shannon stared at him, eyes widened in shock this time. 'If you think for a moment that I'd consider—'

'You didn't hear me out.' He still looked totally relaxed. 'There are good reasons why we should get it together again.'

'Name one!' she demanded, recovering command of some if not all of her senses.

The grey eyes roved her face, taking in every striking detail, dropping to view that part of her unhidden by the table top, lips widening again as his gaze lingered on the thrust of her breasts against the wool of her sweater. 'I'd have thought it was obvious. I still want you, Shannon. I've never stopped wanting you.'

'But I don't want *you*!'

It was an outright lie; the hot rush of blood through her veins, the pounding of her heartbeats in her ears, the tension building inside her were only too indicative of an instant and wholly ungovernable arousal. She came unsteadily to her feet, gripping the table top so tightly, her finger joints showed white, struggling to stay on top of her emotions.

'I wouldn't come back to you if we were the last two people left alive in the world!'

'If we were, you'd have to,' he said, unmoved by the vehemence. 'The only way to repopulate.'

'I'd raid a sperm bank rather than let you anywhere near me!' she clipped, not caring how ridiculous the argument was. 'I always knew you were arrogant, Kyle, but this is one time when you don't get your way!'

'There's such a thing as over-emphasis,' he commented drily. 'A simple no might have been more convincing. As it is…'

He dropped his hands and came to his feet in the same smooth movement, indolence ousted by a purposefulness that hammered Shannon's heart afresh. She backed away as he rounded the table towards her, only to be brought up short as the chair at her back came up against the nearby unit.

'Just stop this!' she ordered. 'Whatever your game is, just stop it *now*!'

'No game,' he said. 'When words fail to make impact, action is the only recourse left.' He caught the fist she swung wildly at his jaw before it could connect, shaking his head in mocking remonstrance. 'Forget the histrionics. This is reality.'

Recognising the futility in further verbal protest, Shannon went deliberately limp as he pulled her into his arms, determined to give him no encouragement. Only, while the mind might be willing, the flesh was decidedly weak, she found, feeling the undoubted thrill run through her as she came into contact with the lean, muscular body. His hands were warm at her back, burning through her clothing to scorch the skin beneath—moving downwards to cup the curves of her buttocks and bring her even closer to his masculine hardness, his eyes watching her face, reading the involuntary reaction.

He lowered his head, mouth just barely brushing hers at first, the movement slow, subtle, tantalising—breaking down her resistance by degrees until she stopped the inner fighting and began blindly to respond, lips softening, opening, moving in accord, body curving to the shape of him, arms sliding about his neck. It had been so long, so very long! She had almost forgotten what it felt like to want with such passionate abandon.

The long, clever fingers found the bottom edge of her sweater, sliding up over tremoring bare flesh. She hadn't bothered to put on a brassière, and her breasts filled his palms, nipples tautened into aching peaks by the skilful, mind-spinning caresses.

Only when he moved his hands down again to ease beneath the elasticated waistband of her leggings did she regain some command of her senses. It took every ounce of will-power she had left to override the craving and grasp both his hands in hers.

'That's enough!' she got out, breath coming hard and fast. 'There's no way you're going any further!'

His own breathing barely ruffled, Kyle gave a low laugh. 'You're quite sure about that?'

'Totally.' From somewhere, Shannon found the strength, both of mind and body, to prise his hands from her, pushing herself jerkily away from him to seize the chair and swing it between them, expression as contemptuous as she could make it. 'As sure as I was the first time you tried that technique of yours on me!'

'Except that you didn't know then what you were missing.' Kyle was making no attempt to thrust the chair aside, the glint in his eyes more suggestive of amusement than frustration. 'No matter. There's time enough. We're going to be stuck here a couple of days, at least—unless there's a mighty swift thaw.'

'It won't make any difference.' Shannon was fast recovering control of herself—on the surface, at any rate. 'If you touch me again, I'll ruin you for life!'

Thumbs hooked casually into pocket tops, Kyle leaned his weight against the nearby unit to regard her with interest. 'And how exactly would you propose doing that?'

'You'll find out if you try it again,' she blustered. 'Just stay away from me!'

'I can hardly do that if we're going to renew our marriage vows,' he said. 'I'm not cut out for celibacy—as you so obviously realise. What you need—'

'What I need is for *you* to take off the way you came!' she flung at him.

He shook his head in mock sorrow, a comma of the thick dark hair falling forward over his forehead. 'Not possible, I'm afraid. As I just said, we're stuck until the snow clears. If you will choose to visit the wilds of Exmoor in February, what would you expect?'

'Hardly the wilds,' Shannon defended, drawn despite herself. 'There's a village only a couple of miles away.'

'May as well be on the moon in these conditions.' He straightened away from the unit, cocking an eyebrow as she jerked the chair onto its two back legs ready to use it as a weapon if he made a move towards her. 'Don't worry, I'm not about to put any more pressure on you.' There was a certain deliberation in the pause, a subtle change of mood. 'Not the same kind, at any rate.'

Shannon put up a shaky hand and brushed back the hair from her face, only now becoming aware that the securing clip had fallen out at some point. 'What's that supposed to mean?'

'I said there were *reasons* why we should get back together.'

She eyed him warily, still not convinced that he wasn't planning on making another grab. 'There's no possible reason you could find that would matter enough, I can tell you that now!'

'Not even if it means my sister's daughter spending the rest of her childhood in an orphanage?'

The question was quiet, the taunting inflection gone from his voice. Totally thrown, Shannon could find no immediate response. There was no doubting his seriousness. His whole demeanour had undergone a radical alteration. She knew that his only sister had died in Australia some years ago, leaving a husband and three-year-old child. She also knew that the father had subsequently cut both himself and the child off from all further contact with the Beaumont family, for reasons Kyle had never gone into.

'I gather something happened to your brother-in-law?' she said confusedly.

'He was killed by a train a few weeks ago. His car got stuck on the line. He didn't get out in time.' Kyle's tone was unemotional. 'Apparently, he didn't have any living relatives of his own, so the authorities out there looked up my sister's records. As my parents are divorced, and both out of the country anyway, that makes me Jodie's only real hope.'

'I see.' Shannon paused, brows drawn together. 'I'm sorry, of course, but I don't really see where I come in.'

'You come in because I plan to adopt her legally, and there's no way a man living alone is going to be allowed custody of a nine-year-old girl who isn't his own daughter. The authorities have to believe I'm in a stable marriage.'

Staring at him, Shannon was aware of a sudden aching void in her stomach. He wanted her back not because he couldn't live without her, but because without her he could be denied care of his sister's child.

'That's blackmail,' she said thickly.

'I know.' He sounded anything but penitent about it, face set in lines she recognised only too well from past encounters. 'I'll use whatever it takes to secure Jodie's future.'

'Regardless of who else might suffer?' Shannon could hardly get the words out through the tightness in her throat. 'Our marriage was over when I found out about you and Paula Frearson. Why should I be expected to put all that aside?'

'Because I'm asking you to. All right—' he held up a hand '—coercing you. As I said before, I'm not going to start going over it all again. It has to be a fresh start.' His tone softened. 'We still have what it takes to make a go of it, Shannon. We just proved that much.'

'You really think I'd ever trust you again?' Her voice was brittle, her whole body trembling with tension.

The grey eyes returned her gaze steadily. 'Did you *ever* really trust me?'

'Of course I did! I wouldn't have married you otherwise.'

'You married me,' he said, 'because I met all the criteria. Don't let's try making out you'd have felt the same way about me if I'd been some nine-to-fiver bringing home a modest salary. You wanted the kind of lifestyle you write about. You wanted a man who could satisfy you in bed, which I don't remember failing to do—or any place else, for that matter.'

'It wasn't like that!' The protest was thick with hurt. 'I was in love with you!'

'You were in love with the idea of it,' he returned inexorably. 'I was your hero figure come to life. A role I was quite willing to play, up to a point, but not for the rest of my life. In some ways, I suppose you could say Paula was *my* bit of escapism.'

'So it was all *my* fault!' Shannon was hard put to it to retain any command at all over her emotions.

'No,' he said. 'A lot of it was mine, for pandering to a fantasy. At least you're seeing me for what I really am now.'

Shannon drew a deep hard breath, her chin lifting as pride came to her rescue. '*That* much you're definitely right about. Which means I hardly see you as an ideal father replacement for your niece.'

A muscle jerked faintly along his jawline, but both gaze and voice remained level. 'I can give her a better life than any orphanage could offer.'

She had to allow fair dues there. One thing Kyle had never been was mean. With him, the child would lack for nothing money could provide. She could appreciate his feelings where Jodie was concerned—even admire him for what he contemplated doing. What she couldn't countenance was his total lack of concern for *her* feelings.

'I'm sorry,' she said roughly, 'but I can't help you.'

'You mean you won't.' He was no longer leaning against the unit, the tautness of his jaw echoed in the line of his mouth.

'I mean I can't.' Shannon forced herself to meet his gaze directly, registering the steely glint with a flutter of nerves already stretched to breaking point. 'I...have other plans,' she got out.

'Such as what exactly?'

'Such as the fact that I'm going to marry another man.'

The laugh was short and brusque. 'Considering biga-my, are you?'

'I'm obviously not talking about tomorrow,' she responded, doing her best to sound sure of what she was saying. 'Craig is quite prepared to wait until I'm free.'

'He'll be waiting a hell of a long time, then!'

Eyes dark, Shannon kept a tight rein on her tongue. 'You can't stop me from divorcing you, Kyle. Any more than you can coerce me into coming back to you. If you need a woman around the house in order to keep Jodie, I'm sure there'll be no shortage of takers. You might even find Paula ready to get back in on the act.'

She left it there because, judging from the expression on the lean features, it would have been tempting providence to go any further. Kyle had never been given to physical violence, but right now he looked close to it, hands driven deep into his pockets as if in order to keep himself from putting them about her neck, eyes like gimlets.

'If you want an easy divorce, you're going to have to work for it,' he clipped. 'You come with me to fetch Jodie, and stay with us until the legalities are taken care of. Once that's done, you can have your divorce uncontested.' He shook his head to the protest forming on her lips, adamancy in every line. 'That's the offer. Three months should about cover it.'

The way things looked right now, three days would be too long, thought Shannon numbly. She had come to the cottage in order to have time to think long and hard about her relationship with Craig, but until a moment ago she had made no hard and fast decision. There was no certainty in it even now, but it was too late to rescind.

'And what am I supposed to tell Craig in the meantime?' she said.

'The truth—providing he keeps it to himself.' Kyle wasn't giving an inch. 'If he cares enough, he'll wait. He'll have to wait! I need you more than he does.'

If only it wasn't just for Jodie's sake, came the aching thought. If only... Shannon closed her mind to the rest. All Kyle really wanted from her was her presence; the move he'd made earlier had been nothing more than a calculated attack on her senses in order to undermine any possible resistance. He'd left her with little choice in the end. It would take a heart far harder than hers to condemn a child to an institution for years. Only there had to be some ground rules laid down first.

'If I go along with this, it will be on the understanding that you keep yourself strictly to yourself,' she stated with grim emphasis. 'Lay another finger on me at any time, and I walk! Is that clear?'

'As crystal.' Whatever his inner feelings, Kyle wasn't revealing them. 'All you have to do is put on a convincing performance of marital harmony when it's called for. The rest of the time...' He paused, gave a shrug. 'You'll just have to put up with me.'

Right now, Shannon had had enough. Her nerves were jangling, her equilibrium shot to pieces.

'I'm going to have a shower,' she declared roughly. 'The guest room is on the left at the top of the stairs, if you want to have a rest after all your exertion getting here.'

She didn't wait for an answer, turning on her heel to walk swiftly from the kitchen and up the stairs.

The bedroom was warm and cosy again, the heavy wooden door a barrier against the world. Her shower forgotten, Shannon subsided onto the bed, lying there gazing unseeingly at the raftered ceiling as her mind started back down the years...

CHAPTER TWO

AS PARTIES went, she'd known better, Shannon reflected, trying to show an intelligent interest in her present companion's self-opinionated discourse. Top-line author he might be; in person he was proving an outstanding bore! She could only hope *she* never became so wrapped up in her own importance.

Not that there was much chance of it, she thought humorously. Despite capturing a major percentage of the market, romantic fiction still tended to be regarded as a bit of a joke by both the media and literary critics alike, the purveyors of it equally so. Written by frustrated middle-aged ladies with nothing much else to do seemed to be the general conjecture.

The man she was talking to—or, more correctly, who was talking at her—was short in stature if not in verbosity. At five feet six in her bare feet, and wearing three-inch heels, she towered over him. Eyes wandering for a moment, she found herself looking directly into an openly amused male face nearby. Although part of a group, he appeared to be paying little attention to the conversation going on around him. Only when the woman by his side touched his arm did he transfer his gaze, the smile he directed enough to give any female with normal reactions palpitations.

Who, Shannon wondered, feeling her own quickened pulse rate, was that? And how was it she hadn't noticed him before this?

The answer had to be obvious: he hadn't been there to notice prior to this. Early thirties, well over six feet in height, hair thick and crisp and dark as night, face so totally, uncompromisingly masculine in its definition, he epitomised her fondest fantasies. No way could she have missed him!

Looks were only half of it, though. No doubt when it came to personality he would prove as big a disappointment as most. Too much brain-washing by the politically correct brigade, that was the trouble. Gone were the days when men were men and women were women, and everyone knew the difference!

Both he and the woman with him had moved on when she risked another glance. So much for the 'across a crowded room' theme, she thought whimsically. Had she been writing the scene, it would have been instant and mutual lust!

She managed eventually to extricate herself with reasonable grace from the bore's company by claiming that she needed to freshen up. If this was the average publishing bash, she told herself, applying lipstick in the cloakroom, it could well be both her first *and* her last. She had better things to do than stand around drinking champagne and buttering up egos—like finishing her present book, for instance. The only time she felt truly fulfilled was when she was writing.

She took a last critical look in the long mirror before leaving the room, tucking a strand of long blonde hair back behind an ear and running a hand down the form-fitting skirt of her black dress to iron out an imaginary wrinkle.

Was her editor right in saying that her heroines were an extension of herself? she mused, viewing the piquant features looking back at her. True, the first three had all had blonde hair, but they'd been very different in character, she was sure. Anyway, she'd given the latest one red hair—with the temper to go with it. Fun to write, and hopefully entertaining to read. Barbara would be the judge.

Heat and noise and smoke met her afresh as she emerged from the room. There was a terrace beyond the double doors over there, she believed. Even allowing for city pollution, the night air had to be of better quality than this. No one was going to miss her if she went out for a few minutes.

The skies were clear, the early April temperature refreshing. Shannon walked to the balustrade to look out over the river, enjoying the coolness on her skin. This time last year her first book had just hit the shelves. Apart from family and friends, the interest had been minimal, but sales had proved good. Under contract now with Newton Mansfield, she could count herself already established. Not bad at twenty-two, she thought, allowing herself a smidgen of complacency.

It had been a gamble, of course, abandoning her career prospects in banking in order to write full-time, but it was paying off, and not just financially. In her books she could escape from all dull day-to-day routine. That was the bonus.

'I've been looking for you,' said a thrillingly deep-timbred voice at her back, contracting every muscle in her stomach and a few more besides. 'Aren't you cold out here?'

Shannon turned her head slowly, somehow knowing who she would see. Up close, he was even more arresting, shoulders wide beneath the superbly cut black jacket. Eyes grey, she registered, nose strong but proportionate, mouth firm, well-shaped, the lower lip revealing a hint of sensuality. He might have stepped straight out of her imagination!

'No,' she said, making a valiant effort to sound normal. 'Not a bit. It's too warm in there, anyway.'

'Hardly surprising, the amount of hot air being generated,' he returned with easy humour. 'You were looking distinctly glassy-eyed the last time I saw you. The effect our Jeremy tends to have on people, I'm afraid.'

'You're with his publishers?' she hazarded, seizing on the 'our'.

'In a manner of speaking.' He had moved up beside her, leaning an elbow on the balustrade, eyes shrewdly assessing as they rested on her face. 'I write for them too.'

'Oh?' She was even more captivated. 'Should I know you?'

'Depends.' He sounded amused. 'I write under James Warren, but the name's Beaumont. Kyle to friends.'

Green eyes widened. This, Shannon thought dazedly, was getting better by the second! 'I've read everything you've written!' she declared, stretching a point. 'You hit the best-seller's list with all your books!'

The dark head inclined in semi-mocking acknowledgement. 'I shouldn't have thought they'd hold all that much appeal for a romantic novelist.'

'Just because I write romance, it doesn't have to follow that it's all I read,' she returned on a slightly tarter note. 'I've even been known to dip into Tolstoy on occasion.'

'No slur on your intelligence level intended.' He wasn't in the least abashed. 'Just very different genres, that's all.'

Already regretting the defensiveness, Shannon decided the best thing to do was ignore it. 'How did you know I write romance, anyway?'

'I made enquiries,' he said. 'Shannon Holroyd; pen name, Sylvia Halston. Set to become one of Newton M's most prolific authors, by all accounts.'

Shannon had to smile. 'I've a long way to go.'

'A long time to do it in.' Kyle was smiling too. 'Twenty-two is pretty young to have made it this far.'

'Thirty-two is pretty young to be where *you* are,' she returned, drawing on what little she could remember of his media profile. 'How come I've never seen a photograph of you?'

He shrugged. 'Probably because I don't like having photographs taken.'

'And what you don't like doing you don't do,' she hazarded. 'That comes dangerously close to temperament.'

'You're coming dangerously close to finding out just how temperamental I can be,' he rejoined with a glint.

'Well, hush my mouth!' Shannon fluttered her eyelashes at him, fingers to lips. 'I'm all of a tremble!'

His laugh was no disappointment either. 'You're all of a provocation, I'll grant you!'

'To what?' she asked innocently, and saw the grey eyes take on silver sparks.

'This,' he said, and drew her to him, finding her mouth with unerring aim.

It was hardly the first time she'd been kissed, but this was different from any she had known before. His lips were smooth, supple, moving lightly, caressingly, easing hers apart, his hands sliding up her arms to seek the warm bare flesh revealed by the scooped out neckline of her dress, thumbs smoothing her collarbone. Shannon was lost in a world of sensation, the blood singing in her ears, every nerve in her body tingling. She wanted, *needed* to be closer—to feel that lean muscularity against her.

What she didn't want was for him to stop. The sense of deprivation when he lifted his head was acute. It took a real effort to conjure up a suitably nonchalant expression.

'Such technique!' she murmured. 'Obviously well-practised.'

He ran the back of his knuckles down her cheek, expression faintly ironic. 'I have my moments. Are you hungry?'

Not for food, she could have told him. 'Starving!' she said.

'So let's get out of here. Dinner first. We'll decide where we go from there.'

Not a man accustomed to having his attentions spurned for certain, Shannon reflected, unable to deny a ripple of excitement at the assertive tone. He wanted her; it was right there in his eyes when he looked at her. He wasn't going to get her, of course, but the knowledge was uplifting in itself. The woman he'd been with in there could knock her into a cocked hat when it came to both looks and sophistication, yet she was the one he'd come after.

'I thought you were already with someone,' she said, seeking affirmation.

Dark brows drew together for a brief moment, then cleared. 'You mean Angela? She's my agent.'

'And you never mix business and pleasure, of course?'

His mouth curved. 'You could say that. Are you going to get your coat?'

Try and stop me! she thought. 'I'd be delighted to have dinner with you,' she said, tongue-in-cheek. 'Thank you for asking me.'

The smile widened. 'You're more than welcome.'

That was how it had all started. Sitting up now, back against the headboard, arms wrapped about bent knees, Shannon wondered what course her life might have taken if she had refused to have dinner with Kyle that night. Would his interest in her have survived the rejection? Maybe she should try asking him—although it made no difference, whatever the answer might be.

To do him credit, he hadn't attempted to get her into bed that first night. Nothing so crude. His campaign had been measured, starting with an all-too-brief parting kiss that had left her yearning for more, developing over the following weeks to a point where she had wanted so badly to give way to him—to experience the full, passionate lovemaking she described in her books but had no real practical knowledge of.

She had held out because she was head over heels in love with him by then, and afraid of losing him once he'd had everything she had to give. Even so, she had never really expected to be marrying him barely two months later...

Due more to Kyle's reputation than to hers, the wedding attracted a lot of media publicity. Shannon was almost glad when it was over, when she could take off the hand-stitched satin bridal gown and romantic floating veil her mother had deemed so essential to the occasion, and get into the pale cream suit she had chosen to go away in.

The reception at Brenton's top hotel had cost her father a packet, she knew, but he had refused to allow her to share in expenses, although she could well have afforded it. No daughter of his was going to pay for her own wedding, he had declared, however much she earned!

He and Kyle had hit it off straight away, despite the age gap. 'A razor-sharp brain, that man of yours,' he'd pronounced after finishing all six published works. 'The amount of technical detail he puts in is phenomenal! I could almost fly a Jumbo jet myself after reading that last one!

'A real strong character too,' he'd added slyly. 'You'll not be able to twist him round your little finger, the way you've always done with me.'

'Dad thinks you're the bee's knees,' she said lightly as her husband emerged from the bathroom, where he'd been removing his five-o'clock shadow.

'And what does his daughter think?' he asked, coming over to slide both arms about her waist from behind and nuzzle his lips into the side of her neck beneath the fall of blonde hair.

'That I'm the luckiest woman alive, what else?' She widened her eyes at him guilelessly in the dressing-table mirror. 'A handsome, wealthy husband, a beautiful country retreat, an apartment in town—what more could there be?'

He gave a slow smile, lifting his hands to cover the swell of her breasts. 'The best is yet to come.'

'Supposing I turn out to be a disappointment?' she murmured, senses tuned to the stimulating caress. 'For all you know, I might even be frigid!'

His laugh was low. 'Not in a million years! Do you think I don't know when a woman is aroused? You've wanted me to make love to you as much as I've wanted it.'

She kept her tone light, bantering, watching his face. 'Would you have married me if I'd slept with you?'

He laughed again, eyes taunting. 'We'll never know, will we?'

It wasn't the answer she had hoped for, but it was all she was obviously going to get. Declarations of undying love weren't his style; she already knew that. She just had to be content with the ring on her finger.

They were to spend the night at a hotel close to the airport before flying out to Bali on honeymoon. Kyle ordered dinner served in the privacy of their room by candlelight. Looking at him across the table as he poured more wine for them both, Shannon wondered if she ought to pinch herself to make sure she really was awake. It was all so perfect!

Too perfect to last, came the fleeting thought, as swiftly discarded. This marriage was going to be the most stable there ever was. Twenty-five years from this night, they would be celebrating their silver wedding!

'To us,' Kyle proposed, lifting his glass. 'May fortune continue to smile!'

'It will,' she declared with soaring confidence. 'It wouldn't dare do anything else!'

His laugh indulged her ebullience. 'A natural born optimist!'

The laughter faded as he regarded her candlelit face and glowing eyes, replaced by an expression that created mayhem with her senses. 'I've waited long enough,' he said softly.

Shannon made no reply, heart thudding against her ribs as he set down the glass and pushed back his chair. Now that the moment was here at last, she was afraid. Not of the act of lovemaking itself, but of failing to satisfy him the way she so desperately wanted to satisfy him. Using her imagination, the way she did in her books, was no substitute for experience in the real world. Kyle had known other women before her, women who probably knew all there was to know about gratifying a man. How could she possibly compete?

The worry vanished the moment he started kissing her, driven out by a far more potent emotion. She kissed him back with mounting hunger, body moving instinctively, invitingly against him, feeling him harden, hearing his breathing roughen, knowing a sudden surge of confidence in her own ability.

He had taken off his jacket earlier. Fingers dextrous,

she unbuttoned his shirt, pushing it open to reveal the broad expanse of his chest and press her lips into the wiry curl of dark hair. His skin was damp, the faint saltiness a stimulation in itself. She inserted the tips of both index fingers beneath his trouser waistband, running them slowly round to the front to undo the clip, wanting to touch him, to know him the way she had never known any man.

He caught her hands before she could explore any further, bringing them up to his mouth to kiss both palms. 'Not yet,' he murmured, and swung her up into his arms, carrying her as if she weighed nothing at all across to the bed to lay her down—peeling off first his own shirt and then her blouse and scanty lace brassière.

Kneeling over her, he lowered his head to take each throbbing nipple by turns in his mouth, playing his tongue over and around them until she thought she would die of sheer sensory pleasure. She was hardly conscious of the rest of her clothing being removed, aware of her nudity only when Kyle ran his hand slowly down the length of her body to seek the hot, moist centre between her thighs.

The possessive, intimate caress inflamed her beyond measure, drawing guttural little sounds from her throat as she moved to his command. Shudder after delicious shudder racked her slender frame, but the relief afforded wasn't enough—not nearly enough.

'More,' she whispered huskily. 'More, more, *more*!'

Kyle laughed deep in his throat, and got to his feet to rid himself of his remaining clothing. Shannon watched him through slitted eyelids, quivering like an aspen leaf. She wasn't naive; she had seen the male body nude before, if only in art form. What she hadn't seen was the fully aroused male.

Too aroused herself to be hesitant, she touched him,

delicately at first, then with increasing confidence as she watched his eyes darken and heard the breath rasp in his throat. He came down to find her mouth with his in a long, deep kiss, body poised while he parted her thighs, then lowering to merge with hers, the incursion controlled, gentle as it was possible to be in forging the passage, his lips smothering her involuntary cry at the fleeting pain, kissing her back to a state where nothing else existed but the wonderful feeling of togetherness.

Whatever pleasure he had afforded her previously, it was nothing compared with the tumult growing in her as he started to move again, the strokes lengthening, quickening, carrying her with him until everything merged into a blur and the world went haywire.

She came back to earth to feel his weight pinioning her, the dark head on her shoulder. Only when she moved did he lift himself on his elbows, looking down at her with a smile playing about his lips.

'How do you feel?' he asked softly.

'Revelated,' she said.

'There's no such word.'

'Well, there should be.' She eased her position a little, eyes widening as she felt the stirring between her thighs. 'Again!'

One dark brow lifted. 'Is that a complaint?'

'No, just surprise,' she admitted. 'I always thought it took more time for a man to…regenerate.'

'Depends on the incentive. With you…' he dropped a kiss on the end of her nose '…it's a foregone conclusion.'

The question was meant to sound light, though it didn't quite succeed. 'Does that mean I was worth waiting for?'

'Infinitely,' he returned with reassuring certainty. 'You're a lovely, sensual, wholly desirable lady, Mrs

Beaumont.' The grey eyes were kindling again. 'With regard to which...'

It was getting light outside, Shannon realised. She glanced at the clock sitting on the bedside table, amazed to see that more than three hours had passed since she had come back upstairs. Having heard no creaking from the wooden treads, she assumed Kyle was still down there. Probably fallen asleep on the sitting-room sofa, she reckoned.

At least it appeared to have stopped snowing, although with what it had put down there would be little chance of digging their way out for a while. Unless she could get through to the farm on the phone, and persuade Mr Lawson to bring his tractor up the lane. Worth a try, at any rate. Anything was better than being stuck here for days under these circumstances!

Not that Kyle was likely to make any further approaches now he had her co-operation. Even if he was telling the truth in saying he still wanted her, it was only a physical desire, which he would have no difficulty in controlling. She wondered if it was lack of any deeper feeling on his side that had finally driven Paula away. Sex could only sustain a relationship for so long, as she knew to her cost...

Those first weeks of marriage were wonderful. Shannon could conceive of no better life than the one she was living. The thronged and highly successful house-warming party they gave was followed by a series of invitations that kept them out almost every night. The ones Kyle would have turned down Shannon insisted on accepting, relishing the envy her capturing of the man so many other women had coveted aroused.

It came as something of a shock the first time Kyle

put his foot down and flatly refused to spend yet another evening in company.

'We need some time on our own,' he said. 'A long, leisurely evening together just listening to music would be heaven.'

Shannon wrinkled her small pert nose. 'We'll have plenty of time for that when we're old and grey! Everyone's going to this party!'

'In which case, we'll hardly be missed.' He shook his head as she opened her mouth to argue that point, his jaw firming. 'We're not going. That's final.'

'So I'll go on my own!' she flashed, resenting the authoritarianism.

Kyle smiled briefly. 'You think I'd let you?'

Her chin tilted. 'You think you can stop me?'

'Definitely.' He reached for her, ignoring her furious protest, a spark in his eyes as he bent his head to find her mouth with unerring aim—kissing her into melting compliance.

'You'd still rather be at the party?' he asked softly a long time later when they lay together before the fire he had lit against the unseasonably cool evening.

'No,' Shannon whispered, too satiated from their lovemaking to think about anything else right now. 'I want to be here with you like this for ever!'

His laugh was low, expression relaxed. 'Your wish is my command!'

That hadn't been the case earlier, came the fleeting thought, ousted before it fully registered by the touch of those long, lean fingers at her breast.

That was far from being their only disagreement. Over the following months, Shannon came to realise just how right her father had been in his assessment of his future son-in-law. Not that she would have wanted a man she could twist around her little finger, but there were times when his intractability in the face of something she wanted to do and he didn't overstepped the mark.

'Marriage is supposed to be about give and take!' she stormed at him once when he declined to spend a weekend boating on the Thames. 'Just because *you* don't happen to like the Mastersons!'

'It isn't a matter of liking or disliking,' Kyle responded levelly. 'We only met them a couple of weeks ago. I'd need to be a lot better acquainted to contemplate sharing close confines on that boat of theirs. Anyway, I'll be working through the weekend.'

'You're always working!'

'Hardly true. I was two months late even starting the book.'

Shannon bit her lip, unable to dispute what she knew to be the truth. Kyle normally submitted a completed manuscript in November for publication the following year, yet here they were in mid-October and he wasn't even halfway through. He wasn't the only one behind with his work either. She should have had a new book finished herself by now.

'Sorry,' she said impulsively. 'I wasn't thinking. Of course you have to work. It's my fault you're not going to meet your deadline this year.'

'You've certainly been a distraction.' He was smiling again, the hand lifting to smooth her cheek tender. 'A very lovely one, though.'

As always, he only had to touch her to set her alight. She loved him so much, she told herself fiercely, meeting his lips. Nothing else mattered but that.

It did, of course, although she made a real effort to moderate her demands on his time during the next few weeks. By Christmas they both had manuscripts finished and despatched, and enjoyed an extended break over the New Year in Barbados, which Kyle planned to use as the opening setting for his next novel. He always allowed himself six months for research, which often included travelling to far-flung places. Having completed another novel herself in the interim, Shannon planned on accompanying him to Thailand in April, and was devastated when he made it plain that he had no intention of letting her.

'I'll be going into places I wouldn't risk taking you,' he said, 'and I wouldn't trust you to stay put in a hotel room on your own for long. I'll only be gone a couple of weeks at the most.'

He remained adamant through all her protests and promises, shrugging resignedly when she refused to come to the airport with him. Shannon spent the two weeks at the London apartment, out on the town almost every evening, mostly with a group of friends, once with an old boyfriend whose interest she found a balm to her wounded spirit. Not that she could honestly claim to have enjoyed herself all that much. Without Kyle there, even champagne tasted flat.

By the time he arrived home she was ready to be the most compliant, understanding wife any man ever had. Feeling his arms about her again, his lips on hers was sheer ecstasy. The euphoria lasted for three whole days, until someone saw fit to advise him of what she had been up to while he'd been away. In the row that followed they both said hurtful things, but what reckoned most with Shannon was his assertion that he should have known better than to marry a spoiled brat like her.

It was from then that things began falling apart between them. His suggestion that they think about starting a family she rejected out of hand on the grounds that she had no intention of being tied down with a baby at her age. Something he should have thought of before, she retorted when he pointed out that, at thirty-three, he needed to be considering fatherhood now, not some indefinite time in the future.

The suspicion that there was another woman in his life grew gradually, although she had no direct evidence to go on. She began picking rows with him, generally acting the termagant, frustrated by his refusal to be drawn into a state of mind where he might let something out.

He was away for a few days when confirmation finally came in the shape of a letter from a Paula Frearson suggesting that she give him his freedom in order for him to marry the woman he should have married in the first place. By the time he returned, Shannon had packed her bags and moved back to her parents' home. She refused to believe anything he had to say when he came to find her, and after several attempts to persuade her into coming back he gave up even trying.

If he'd slung her over a shoulder and carried her off by force, she might have been convinced that he really wanted her back, Shannon reflected wryly, returning to the present. It was what she had waited for—what she had longed for him to do. Only he hadn't, and she'd had to face the fact that the marriage was to all intents and purposes over.

By avoiding the functions at which he might be present, she had managed not to actually see him again since. Financial support had been offered, and turned down; she had neither needed nor wanted any dependence on him. She had organised her life as a single woman, buying a flat of her own and enjoying casual relationships, but what she had never been able to do was put him completely out of mind and heart. Getting involved with him again in any sense was inviting disaster.

It was gone nine, and as light as it was going to get,

when she finally geared herself into venturing downstairs again. Kyle was ensconced on the sitting-room sofa as she had anticipated, but not asleep. He looked up from the paperback book he was perusing to flick a deceptively lazy glance over her as she hovered in the doorway.

'Long shower,' he commented drily.

'I had a sleep first,' she lied, advancing into the room. 'If you want to shave, there's plenty of hot water left. That's assuming you came prepared for an overnight stay, of course?'

'I came prepared for whatever,' he said with purpose. 'Including a refractory wife.'

'I already agreed to what you're asking,' Shannon pointed out. 'That hardly makes me unmanageable.'

'What it makes you is unpredictable all of a sudden,' he admitted. 'I think you might have done some growing up since we last met.'

'If growing up means having learned to tell the difference between lust and love, you might be right,' she agreed shortly. 'That's one mistake I'll never make again.'

He studied her with a certain cynicism, gaze moving down the slender, shapely length of her body and back to her face in slow and reminiscent appraisal, raising flags of colour in her cheeks. 'Can this Craig turn you on the way I could?'

Not in a million years! would have been the truthful answer, but one she had no intention of giving. 'Craig is as different from you as chalk from cheese!' she said with scornful inflection.

'Meaning no, he can't.' The dark head moved in mocking commiseration. 'I'd think twice before marrying someone who fails in that department.'

Temper rising, Shannon fought to keep her end up. 'Perhaps I've changed in *that* department myself!'

Too late, she remembered her response to him earlier, aware from the smile that crossed the lean features that he most certainly hadn't forgotten it.

'Perhaps I'm the only one who *can* turn you on to any extent,' he suggested with a taunting glint in his eyes. 'A one-man woman all the way!'

'If there was any chance of it, I'd shoot myself,' she retorted, blanking out the very real possibility that he was right. 'Keep this up, and you're going to find yourself tackling the authorities on your own,' she added hardily. 'There's a limit to how much I'll take from you, even for your niece's sake.'

'Point taken.' He sounded unperturbed. 'Why don't you sit down and relax—considering that there isn't much else to be done for the present? Maybe read a book? There's a good selection on the shelves over there. Your aunt appears to have very wide-ranging tastes.'

Totally relaxed himself, he picked up the paperback again, for the first time displaying the front cover. One of hers, Shannon realised in mingled surprise and dissension.

'Give me that!' she demanded. 'You're not reading it—you know you're not!'

Kyle glanced across at her with lifted brows, then down again at the open book. 'I'd say I was pretty well advanced at page 127 for someone not reading.'

'You just opened it there to get at me,' she accused. 'You never attempted to read a book of mine through before!'

'Well, maybe I should have done,' he said. 'It might have given me a better insight into what makes you tick. This is one of your early ones—the second, I think. Well-written for a beginner, although your sex scenes lack a certain impact. Not really to be wondered at considering you'd never experienced what you were describing at the time, of course. Now, your later efforts...'

'Written after you taught me everything you know!' she sneered, only just controlling the urge to snatch the book from him. 'Maybe I should offer you a percentage for the instruction!'

His laugh was unexpected, the gleam in his eyes pure devilment. 'Now that would be a real turn up for the books!'

Angered by his very lack of anger at the dig, Shannon gave way to impulse and went for him, knocking the book from his hands with a vicious swipe that left the corner of the page he had been in the process of turning in his fingers. Next moment she was lying half on top of him, his hands hard where they grasped her wrists, face inches from hers.

'If we're going to play rough,' he said softly, 'I'm your man!'

This close, she could feel his breath on her cheek, see the silvery flecks in his eyes, the fine laughter lines radiating away from them. Her breasts were pressing into his chest, the hardness painful yet stimulating too. She wanted badly to put her lips to his and feel the firmness give. Only if she did that, who knew where it might end? The last thing she needed was to be drawn down that path again.

'Just leave my books alone from now on,' she got out, voice low and husky. 'Your opinions are of no importance to me!'

'If that was true, you wouldn't be where you are right now, looking as though you'd like to stick a knife between my ribs,' Kyle responded, making no attempt to release her. 'I wasn't criticising your work. Of its kind, it's very well done.'

He let go of her wrists, but only to run his fingers into the thickness of her hair, his eyes on the soft vulnerability of her mouth as he drew her an inch or so closer still. Shannon could almost feel the prickle of his beard on her skin, and knew a growing temptation just to let go and let matters take their natural course. She wanted him as much as she had ever wanted him—probably more, because she had been deprived for so long.

Only if she did give way, where did that leave her? Once he had the legalities concerning his niece taken care of, there would be nothing to hold them together. Sex he could get from any woman who made herself available the way she was on the verge of doing right now.

'Get your filthy hands off me!' she said between clenched teeth. *'Now!'*

For a suspended moment it was touch-and-go, the grey eyes dangerously lit, then he shrugged and let her slide through his hands, mouth derisive. 'Dialogue hardly up to your usual standard, darling.'

Shannon pushed herself to her feet, unsurprised to find herself unsteady. 'Effective enough, anyway,' she said with taut control. 'Next time you lay your hands on me—'

'I know—you'll ruin me for life!' The derision had increased. 'I'll bear it in mind.' He came lithely upright, directing a mocking glance at her as she took an involuntary step backwards. 'Stop jumping. I'm going to make use of some of that hot water. A shave, a shower and I'll be a new man.'

'Anything would have to be an improvement on the old one,' was the best she could manage, which in retrospect would have been better left unsaid. 'I'm going to ring the farm and see if they'll come down and clear the lane,' she added, before Kyle could make any further comment. 'The sooner we get away from here the better.'

'From every aspect,' he agreed. 'I told them we'd be in Brisbane within the week.'

Eyes darkened, she said thickly, 'Supposing I'd refused?'

'I knew you didn't have it in you,' he said. 'Not with a child's future at stake.' There was a certain deliberation in the pause. 'Maybe things would have been different if we'd had a child ourselves.'

Shannon hardened her heart against the swift, sharp stab. 'You mean something to keep me occupied while you indulged yourself with Paula—or whoever else you took a fancy to?'

If there had been any softening at all about the lean features, it had vanished again. His shrug was dismissive. 'Obviously not. I'll leave you to it, then.'

Shannon sank nervelessly to a seat as he went from the room, only now acknowledging just how much these last few hours had taken out of her. Despite all that had happened, Kyle could still spin the world about her head with just a touch.

Considering which, the chances of her holding out against him for three whole months should he launch any really concentrated assault on her will-power were limited, to say the least. What she had to decide was whether she dared run the risk of falling hook, line and sinker for him again.

CHAPTER THREE

THEY left the cottage early that afternoon, driving in convoy with Kyle leading the way in the Range Rover. Mr Lawson had directed his lad to clear a passage all the way through to the main road, where they found traffic was moving almost normally.

Providing they came up against no major delays, they should, Shannon calculated, be home by six. Her home, that was. Kyle had insisted on accompanying her there before making for his own place. They had arrangements still to make, he'd said.

The decision had been inevitable, of course. There was no way she could jeopardise Jodie's future. With regard to the rest, she would just have to keep a tight rein on herself. Kyle would hardly force the issue.

Breaking the news to Craig was going to be the most difficult part. While he might appreciate the motive, he couldn't possibly be expected to like the idea of her moving back in with her husband, even for a finite period.

How Kyle was going to cope with the child on his own once the adoption was approved was another matter. She doubted if he spent very much of his time at the house, and a London apartment was no place for a child to grow up in.

His problem, anyway, she told herself firmly at that point, but the concern still lingered.

As it turned out, it was gone seven when they finally reached Hampstead. Apart from one brief period, Shannon had managed to keep within sight of the Range

Rover, and was right behind it at journey's end. Her flat was on the second floor of one of the big old houses overlooking the Heath. It was really a little on the large side for one person, but she could afford it, and relished the space.

'I wasn't sure you'd be able to find it, never having been here before,' she said on the way in.

'I know the area,' Kyle returned easily. 'I've a friend who lives not far away.'

Shannon slanted him a glance. 'Anyone I know?'

'Doubtful. He only got back from a four-year stint in the States a few months ago. Brought a wife back with him too. Typical American: good to look at, and independent as they come.'

'Just your type,' Shannon murmured, and received a dry smile.

'No chance. She's as wild about Brady as he is about her. Remember what that feels like?'

She pressed the lift floor button, hoping her face didn't reveal what she was feeling right this minute. 'My memory isn't that good.'

'Mine is.' He said it softly, reminiscently. 'I remember the way you were on our wedding night. How many men in this day and age find themselves a genuine virgin bride?' His tone hardened again, eyes suddenly cool as they rested on her face. 'How many men have had you since?'

None, she could have said with perfect truth, but she doubted if he would believe it even if he heard it.

'None of your business,' she said instead, voice surprisingly steady. 'Any more than your affairs are my business these days. We're getting a divorce when this is over—remember?'

'Oh, yes, you're going to marry this Craig, of course. And what does *he* do for a living?'

The lift came to a stop. Shannon slid open the grilled door, keeping her face averted. 'He's a chartered accountant.'

'Oh, very solid!'

'You can mock all you like,' she said crisply. 'At least with him I know exactly where I am.'

'I was under the impression that you knew exactly where you were with me,' Kyle responded on an ironical note. 'But we can all of us come up with the occasional surprise.'

After this, she wouldn't be surprised at anything *he* came up with, she thought caustically, fitting her key in the lock.

Decorated in dark blue and cream with a deep red carpet to add warmth, the hall had five doors leading from it. Shannon opened the first on the right, switching on a light as she entered to reveal a large square living room in which the same rich red was repeated in the drapes at the two tall windows. The furnishings she had picked up here and there as the fancy took her, combining old and not so old to create an atmosphere that was both stylish and comfortable.

'Nice,' Kyle approved, looking round.

'Glad you like it.' She slipped off her tweed coat, long and slender in the matching trousers and black polo-necked sweater belted low on the hip. 'Give me yours,' she added, indicating his leather jacket, 'and I'll go make some coffee. Unless you'd prefer something stronger?'

He shook his head. 'Coffee will be fine. So will the jacket,' he said, sliding out of it and slinging it carelessly over a chair-arm. 'I'm hardly going to be here long enough to warrant hanging it away.'

Shannon smothered an irrational sense of let-down. Once they had the actual detail concerning the coming journey worked out it would be better all round if he left. She had calls to make—one in particular.

Still wearing the same white sweater and jeans, with the shadow showing once more about his jawline, Kyle looked very little different from the morning, but he had to be tired by now, having been up all night. After being on the road for four hours she was weary herself.

'Is it strictly necessary that I come with you to fetch Jodie back?' she asked, hesitating in the doorway. 'I mean, providing you can show your marriage certificate then surely the authorities out there can't put up any objections. Not that it's their concern anyway, I'd have thought, if Jodie's still registered as a British citizen. That's right, isn't it? Your brother-in-law never took naturalisation?'

'Apparently not,' he said. 'Although they'd hardly have thrown Jodie on the streets if she'd had no kin left at all. And yes,' he added as Shannon opened her mouth to reiterate the initial question, 'it is necessary for you to come with me—if only for Jodie's sake. Can you imagine what it would be like for a nine-year-old who recently lost her only parent to be picked up and carted away by a total stranger?'

'But she won't know me either,' Shannon pointed out.

'Much as I hate stating the obvious, you're a woman,' he returned drily. 'That has to give you an edge when it comes to instilling confidence in a little girl. In any case, the flights are already booked.'

Green eyes darkened. 'Arrogant as ever! It wouldn't have occurred to you that I might say no, of course!'

'Not in this case,' he agreed, unmoved by the accusation. 'Whatever faults you might have, callousness isn't among them.'

'If we're going to talk about faults,' she retorted, temporarily sidetracked, 'I could spend all night listing *yours*!'

The sudden grin was disarming. 'I'm sure of it. Words you were never short of. Supposing you make that coffee first? I'm in dire need of a pick-me-up.'

Shannon bit back any further invective, recognising the futility in attempting to get through that skin of his when he was determined not to let her.

'I could get you something to eat, if you like,' she offered with diffidence, not at all sure what she had in stock to give him should he say yes.

He shook his head. 'I'm past hunger. The coffee will do fine—when I finally get it.'

'Someone should tell you,' she rejoined smartly, 'that sarcasm is the lowest form of wit!'

'You just did,' he said as she continued out of the door.

Trust him to have the last word, Shannon fumed. But then what was new? He'd always been able to flatten her.

She percolated the coffee instead of settling for instant as she probably would have done had she been alone. Carrying the tray through, she found Kyle comfortably settled in one of the deep club chairs, but it wasn't until she set the tray down on a table that she realised he was asleep.

Even in repose his features lost nothing of their firmness, the skin stretched taut over hard male cheekbones, mouth closed, jaw in line. His breathing was steady, audible but not overloud. Shannon had heard other women complain about their partner's snoring keeping them awake, but Kyle had never snored, no matter which position he slept in.

Studying him now, she felt the same overwhelming emotions he had always aroused in her. Physical attraction was only a part of it; if he lost his looks he would still exert the same power by the very nature of his personality.

He stirred, murmuring something she couldn't quite catch but which sounded short enough to be a name. Not hers for certain, she thought, hardening her heart.

Extending a foot, she none too gently nudged one of his. 'Coffee up!'

The grey eyes opened with reluctance. 'Do that again,' he growled, 'and I'll not be answerable!'

'I don't need do it again,' she said coolly. 'You're awake. I thought you'd want the coffee before it went cold. Apart from which, we have things to discuss— although I fail to see quite what, considering you're such a forward planner.'

'What was it you were saying about sarcasm?' he asked, sitting up to take the cup she had poured. He drank half the contents at one swallow, and nodded appreciatively. 'You can still make coffee!'

One of the few kitchen things she had been able to do right, Shannon took that to mean. She let the comment pass. It was only the truth, when all was said and done. Her suggestion in the first month of marriage that they employ a full-time housekeeper had been met with an outright refusal to even contemplate it. With daily help to keep the house spick and span, and a husband who had no objection to taking his turn at meal preparation when required, why would a housekeeper be needed? he'd said. All she had to do was learn to cook.

Well, she hadn't then and she hadn't now. Even Craig, loyal as he was, had opted for eating out whenever possible. Kyle had never once railed at her for failing to become a cordon bleu cook, she had to admit. More often than not, they'd eaten out too.

So what? she asked herself defensively. There was more to life than cooking!

'So when exactly are we flying?' she asked, taking a seat as far away as possible.

'Thursday night, arriving in Brisbane early Saturday morning, their time. I've set up a meeting for Saturday afternoon at the home where Jodie is being looked after. That will give us time to turn ourselves round first.'

A whole four or five hours after flying halfway round the world! Shannon reflected with irony, but refrained from voicing the thought.

'Assuming you also booked return flights, how long will we be there? I'd like to give Craig some idea of when I'll be back in the country again.'

Kyle returned her gaze without a flicker. 'I didn't book return flights yet. There's no knowing how long it's going to take to get the paperwork done. Sure to be some. Bureaucracy isn't confined to England.'

Sensing the protest hovering on her lips, he added smoothly, 'Phone your Craig now if you like, and I'll do the explaining for you.'

'You'd enjoy that, wouldn't you?' Eyes stormy, Shannon was in no mood for soft-pedalling. '"I'm taking my wife to the other side of the world and I can't say when we'll be back, so hard cheese!" If you think—'

She broke off there because Kyle was laughing, his whole face breaking up with it. 'The dialogue's going downhill fast, honey! *Hard cheese?*'

'Go to hell!' she said furiously, too angry to see the funny side herself. 'I'm not going anywhere with you, you louse! You can get out of here right now!'

The humour was wiped from his face to be replaced by a dangerous austerity. He placed the cup and saucer on the table with deliberation, obviously weighing his words.

'Having already agreed, you're not only coming with me,' he declared, 'but you're going to put your all into convincing the authorities here that we're suitable parents for Jodie. Any doubts, and they can still take her away, niece or not. The child's interests have to come first. That's something you might consider.'

Unable to hold the steel-hard gaze, Shannon looked down at the hands locked tight together in her lap, teeth catching at her lower lip. He was right, of course: Jodie was more important than any wounded feelings.

'I'll ring Craig when you've gone,' she said with what composure she could muster, unable to bring herself to voice any kind of apology. 'I've a lot to do if I'm to get myself organised by Thursday.' She looked up again, eyes widening as realisation struck home. 'That's the day after tomorrow!'

'That's right.' If he was still angry it wasn't showing. His face was expressionless. 'You'll need a visa, which means visiting Australia House personally, considering the short notice. I'll pick you up at ten. You can fit in anything you need from town at the same time.'

He had come to his feet as he was speaking. Reaching for the jacket he had slung over the chair-arm, he slipped it on, zipping it halfway. The white sweater made his jaw look even darker than it was. He had always, Shannon remembered, been a twice-a-day man. Too much testosterone, that was half the trouble!

'Supposing we really had been stuck at the cottage a couple of days?' she said. 'You didn't leave much leeway at the best.'

His shrug was brief. 'If I'd had to reschedule I'd have rescheduled. Try and confine yourself to a carry-on, will you? That way we don't waste time hanging around carousels.'

What he meant was that *he* had no intention of hanging around carousels, she surmised. With no idea of how long a stay to cater for, it would have to be a pretty spacious carry-on, although they were hardly likely to need anything dressy. Hopefully, bureaucracy would move a little faster over there.

She accompanied him to the outer door in order to lock it when he'd left—or so she told herself. It was only when he reached out a hand to slide it about her neck and draw her closer that she acknowledged her true reason. Regardless of anything and everything she wanted him to kiss her again: her whole body was fired with the need to feel his lips on hers.

For a timeless moment he studied her upturned face, the expression in his eyes sending tremors the length of her spine.

'One more thing,' he said softly. 'Don't call me a louse again.'

He was gone before she could summon a reply—if there was any reply to be made. Closing the door, she leaned against it with eyes closed, doing her best to cope with her warring emotions. He had known what was in her mind just then; he couldn't have failed to know. He'd been on the verge of obliging her too, she was sure, but he had chosen to abstain for reasons best known to himself.

Perhaps he'd come to the conclusion that the only way they were going to get through this was by keeping a physical distance between them. She could see the sense in that arrangement, even though her body disputed it.

Whatever else was missing, the sheer animal attraction was as strong as it ever was. Kisses could, and probably would, lead to other things, with all the subsequent complications. She owed Craig better than that. She owed *herself* better than that.

It was still only just gone eight. If she was going to tell Craig at all—which she could hardly not do—it had better be sooner rather than later. Explaining the situation was going to be one of the most difficult things she had ever done. Craig could hardly be expected to take it lightly. While he might not be able to arouse quite the same passions in her that Kyle could, what she felt for him was worth a great deal more in the long run. The last thing she wanted to do was hurt him.

Mentally girding up her loins, she went to the telephone, drawn by the flashing red light on the answering machine to rewind the tape for playback before making the call. There was only the one message, and it was from Craig himself:

'I tried to reach you at the cottage. Guessed you must be on your way home because of the weather. I'm on the six-thirty to Frankfurt. Problems. Hoping to be back Friday, but if it looks like going over the weekend I'll ring you.' The precise delivery gave way to a softer note. 'Hope you came to the right conclusions.'

Shannon stood for an irresolute moment or two, wondering how best to handle this new complication. It was too late to phone his office to find out whereabouts he was staying in Frankfurt, though she could, if necessary, get in touch with someone who would know. The question was, would it be fair to land this on him when he was obviously going to need to give his undivided attention to the job in hand?

The answer to that, she decided, had to be no. Which left her with the dilemma of when exactly she *was* going to be able to tell him the story. Even if he did get back on Friday, she would be long gone.

Putting it all down in a letter to be waiting for him

whenever he did get back might be the best idea. She could choose her words so much more carefully on paper. A bit of a cop-out, perhaps, but what other choice did she have? It wasn't as if she would be telling him she didn't want to see him again. All she wanted was his understanding.

That just left her parents. They had to be put in the picture, of course. Only not tonight; she just couldn't face her mother's disappointment when it was realised that the arrangement would only be temporary. Tomorrow would be soon enough.

Kyle arrived promptly at ten looking a great deal more rested than Shannon felt herself. She had spent most of the night tossing and turning, unable to turn off the emotional conflict. In eighteen months she had never fully subdued the craving for bodily contact in bed. There had been times when she had been tempted to allow Craig to spend the night simply to feel a man's arms about her again. The only thing holding her back had been the knowledge that it wasn't just *any* man's arms she was missing.

'What did you tell your parents?' Kyle asked when they were in the car.

'Nothing yet,' she admitted. 'It's a difficult situation to explain.'

'You can hardly keep it a secret for three months.' He braked down for the traffic lights ahead, accelerating again as they changed to green. 'Do they know about Craig?'

'Of course.'

'I mean that you're planning to marry him.'

Shannon hesitated. 'Not yet.'

'A recent decision, then.' The firm mouth took on a sardonic line. 'Like yesterday morning, for instance?'

Her chin lifted sharply. 'I'd made up my mind before you arrived on the scene.'

'You didn't need time to make up your mind about marrying me, from what I recall.'

Shannon swallowed on the hard dry lump that rose suddenly in her throat. 'One learns from one's mistakes.'

'Does one?' he mocked. 'It won't last. I can tell you that now.'

'Considering you've never even met Craig, you can't tell me anything,' she clipped back. 'He has qualities you wouldn't even begin to understand!'

'But he can't give you satisfaction where it matters.'

'You think you're the only one capable of that?'

'I'm capable of recognising sexual starvation in a woman.'

'You knowing so much about women, of course!' she jerked out.

The grey eyes turned briefly her way. 'I know *you*.'

Shannon exerted every ounce of control she possessed to keep both face and voice from reflecting the emotions running riot inside her. 'No, you don't. I'm not the *ingénue* you married any more. I admire what you're doing for your sister's child, and I'll see the adoption through, but that's as far as it goes.'

Broad shoulders lifted. 'As you say.'

The traffic was starting to build up. Shannon left him to concentrate on the road, leaning her head back against the rest and closing her eyes. It was going to take all her resilience to get through the coming three months without giving way to what Kyle could still so easily make her feel. Even now, not touching him in any way, she was aware with every fibre of his lean length. Sexual starvation, he had called it, but it was more than just sex she was starved of.

It took longer than anticipated to secure the visa. The morning had flown by the time they were through.

They went to Rules for lunch, Kyle having already reserved a table. Given a choice, Shannon would have opted for somewhere they were unlikely to run into anyone they knew—although it was doubtful if they were going to be able to keep the apparent reconciliation a secret for long, she supposed.

If word did get around, it certainly wasn't going to make things any easier for Craig—especially when it came to picking up their relationship again at the end of the three months. It would be a real test of the strength of his feelings for her.

'Where do you plan on making your main base once everything's settled?' she asked when they'd ordered.

'The house, naturally,' Kyle confirmed. 'The apartment's a long way from the ideal home for a nine-year-old.'

'You'll be employing someone to look after her when I've gone, then.'

He regarded her levelly. 'What makes you think I'll need to?'

Shannon lifted meaningful brows. 'You'll find your social life seriously curtailed if you don't. A nine-year-old can hardly be left on her own of an evening.'

'I dare say Mrs Parkin would stay over if asked—especially as she doesn't have anyone she needs to be home for.'

'I didn't realise you'd kept her on.'

He shrugged. 'The house still needs keeping up to scratch.'

'It's going to make things awkward, though, isn't it?' she said after a moment. 'Our occupying separate rooms, for one thing.'

The grey eyes acquired a mocking glint. 'There's a simple enough solution.'

She curled a deliberated lip. 'You already know the answer to that.'

'I know what you've said. It isn't the way you feel.'

'Stop trying to tell me what I feel!' she flung at him furiously. 'You wouldn't have…'

The arrival of the wine waiter cut short what she had been about to say. Face impassive, the man went through the ritual. He would have heard far worse, Shannon assured herself, but felt no better for it. This was neither the time nor the place for disputes.

'Can we find a neutral subject?' she asked when the man had gone.

Kyle considered her with mock gravity. 'I hear there's a lot of flu about.'

Anger gave way to involuntary laughter. 'I meant a sensible one!'

'There's nothing frivolous about flu. I had a bout myself before Christmas.' His lips curved. 'I could have done with you around then to mop my fevered brow.'

There would have been no shortage of willing hands, Shannon was sure. She said lightly, 'You seem to have made a full recovery.'

'I'd hope so. It's going on for three months ago.'

That figure seemed to be haunting her, came the fleeting thought. She studied him as he lifted his glass to take a drink, wondering just how ill he had really been. She had suffered a bout of influenza herself one year, and wouldn't wish the experience on anybody. It was difficult to imagine that muscular body lying in bed drained of strength and vitality, but that was the effect the bug usually had. It had been several weeks, she remembered, before she had felt truly fit again.

'Let's hope you don't go down with it again this winter,' she said. 'I don't think I could handle the situation on my own.' She paused, hesitant about bringing the subject up. 'You know, you've never said a great deal about your sister. All I know is her name was Janine, and she wasn't very old when she died.'

'Twenty-four.' The grey eyes were unrevealing. 'She was only just twenty-one when she married Trevor and went with him to Australia. Jodie was born seven months later—not, I might add, prematurely.'

'I...see.'

'I doubt if you do,' he said drily. 'The first we knew of any of it was by letter from Brisbane. She was supposed to be visiting friends in France.'

'You'd never met Trevor?'

'A couple of times.'

'But you didn't like him?'

The shrug was brief. 'He wasn't what any of us would have chosen for her, but I dare say we might have worked round it given the opportunity.'

'I suppose with a baby on the way, and knowing how you felt about him, she saw a totally new start as the best solution for everyone,' Shannon hazarded. 'I imagine you didn't leave it at that, though?'

'I went out to see her, yes.'

'*Just* you?'

'My parents were already in the process of separating. They had other things on their minds. Not that it would have done much good anyway. She was totally besotted with the man.'

'Perhaps,' Shannon ventured, 'he had more about him than you thought.'

Kyle gave a short laugh. 'If he did, he kept it well hidden. Janine would have stood a good chance of recovering from the virus that killed her if Trevor had got her medical attention right away. By the time he did get round to it—' He broke off, jaw contracting. 'There wasn't a lot to be done when he refused us any further contact with Jodie. He was in a reasonably good job, and earning enough to pay for someone to look after her during the day, so it seemed best not to subject her to any tug-of-war.'

'Only you blame yourself for leaving it at that,' said Shannon softly, reading between the lines.

'To a great extent, yes. I should have kept tabs on her, if only via an agency.'

'You're making up for it now, doing what you're doing.'

'The very least I can do.'

More than many men his age would even contemplate, she could have said with some truth. Reconciling this present image with the one she had held for the past eighteen months was far from easy. It just went to show how little she really knew him.

'Well, hello there!' exclaimed a voice, and Shannon jerked her head round to see one of their fellow novelists viewing the two of them with avid interest. 'How are you both doing?'

'Extremely well,' said Kyle before Shannon could form an answer. 'Couldn't be better, in fact.'

The interest grew. 'If that means you're back together again, I'm delighted for you both! I assume it's no secret?'

'Not any more.' Kyle was smiling, ignoring the kick Shannon aimed at his ankle under the table. 'Thanks. We're delighted too.'

'You'd no right to do that!' Shannon berated as the other woman went on her way.

'It was what she wanted to hear,' he returned imperturbably. 'I never like to disappoint a lady.'

The tart rejoinder trembling on her lips was bitten

back. 'It's a purely temporary arrangement,' she substituted with emphasis. 'Don't run away with the idea that you're going to talk me into anything more than that!'

'I wouldn't rely on talking you into anything.' He raised his glass, smile taunting. *'Bon appétit!'*

CHAPTER FOUR

THE flight was long and boring. By the time they reached the city-centre hotel after a six-mile taxi ride from the airport, Shannon was too jet-lagged to give much thought to the question of accommodation. Kyle got round the problem by booking a two-bedroom suite.

'Why don't you go and get your head down for a few hours?' he suggested when they reached it. 'I'll inform the home that we've arrived, then probably do the same. We're not due there until three.'

The way she felt, three o'clock the following afternoon would be too soon, Shannon could have told him, but even that was too much trouble.

She took herself off into one of the bedrooms, only pausing to strip off her suit jacket before collapsing onto the wide bed with a heartfelt sigh of relief. It was always worse travelling east: something to do with the magnetic poles, she believed. One hell of a journey to make without stop-overs. One hell of a reason for making it at all, come to that.

She awoke to see light filtering through slatted blinds, and for a second or two couldn't understand where she was.

There was a clock on the bedside table, with the digital display showing 13.43. Memory returned in a rush. She was in Brisbane, Australia, with Kyle. In a little more than an hour they were due to meet the little girl they had come to take back to England.

Pressing herself reluctantly upright, she took a brief look about the room. Up-market, of course; Kyle was hardly going to book them into a flea-pit. The air-conditioning kept the atmosphere so beautifully cool—unlike outside, which had been hot and humid even at the hour they'd arrived. February was high summer here, of course.

It took a real effort to get to her feet. She felt disorientated, her head full of cotton wool. A shower would probably go a long way towards restoring her. Something had to if she was to make that appointment without falling asleep again.

The wardrobes ranged along one wall had full-length mirrors set into all three doors. Seeing herself outlined there, Shannon gave a groan. Her suit skirt was a wrinkled mess, her blouse equally so. Mascara had smudged about her eyes, giving her a distinctly panda-like appearance, while her hair looked like a haystack, with bits sticking out in all directions. Her heroines never woke up looking like this, whatever the circumstances!

If the door over there was the one she had come in by the other one would be the bathroom, she figured. Shared with the other bedroom, no doubt. She could hear no sound. Maybe Kyle was sleeping himself. He would need to get a move on if they were to make the three o'clock appointment he had spoken of.

Stripped, she wrapped herself in the towelling robe provided, and went with her toilet bag to listen for a brief moment at the bathroom door before tentatively opening it. The room was empty, as she had anticipated, the handbowl showing no signs of having been used. If there were no signs of life by the time she finished showering, she would have to go and wake him herself.

Showered, and feeling almost human again, she put the robe back on, then moved across to listen this time at the far door.

A tap brought no response, making her doubt that

Kyle was in the bedroom at all. To make sure, she quietly opened the door and looked through, disconcerted to see him lying face down across one of the two king-sized beds.

So far as she could tell, he was naked, the sheet laid across his waist, one arm hanging over the bed-edge with his fingertips brushing the floor. His head was turned away from her, hair a crisp clean line at his nape.

Muscle rippled across the top of his shoulders as he shifted position, extending down the bronzed, tapering line of his back. The thin sheet left little to the imagination, moulding itself to the firm male contours in a manner that brought a sudden dryness to Shannon's throat, a stirring in the pit of her stomach.

Almost without volition, she went over, putting out a hand to touch the swell of his bicep, tremoring at the smooth, warm feel of his skin. Her fingers curved instinctively to follow the muscular line with a feather-light touch, her lips parting to allow the tip of her tongue to dampen the parched surfaces as the yearning built in her.

He took her completely by surprise when he rolled over. Both arms came up to pull her down to him, his mouth seeking hers with a purpose she couldn't have avoided even if she'd had a chance to try. He rolled again, this time pinning her half beneath him, the sheet trapped between them.

Her robe had parted, held only by the belt about her waist from coming open all the way down. She felt his hand at her breast, his touch like fire on the sensitive flesh, covering, caressing, making her groan in anguish against his lips at the sheer torment.

'Don't!' she managed to gasp. 'Kyle...no!'

'Why not?' he said roughly. 'It's what you want—

what we both want! Why deny what's so patently obvious?'

'I'm not denying it.' Gazing straight into the flame-lit grey eyes, Shannon was hard put to it to achieve an even remotely steady tone. Her breath was coming short and hard, her body responding to him despite all she could do to control it. 'Wanting is one thing,' she managed, 'doing quite another. If you want me to continue helping you with this adoption, you'll stop this right now!'

'*I* wasn't the one who started it,' he pointed out. 'If you didn't want this to happen, you shouldn't have touched me the way you did. How the devil did you expect me to react?'

'I thought you were asleep,' she began, and saw his lips twist.

'So I was, until then.' He rubbed her nipple gently between finger and thumb, the irony increasing as he watched her eyes glaze, her teeth come together. 'I wonder how much more it would take to make you let go?'

Not very much at all, she thought desperately. It was now, in fact, or never! Steeling herself, she jabbed a forearm against his throat, taking advantage of his momentary recoil to tear herself free, the impetus tumbling her to the floor at the side of the bed.

Supporting himself on an elbow, his free hand rubbing his throat, Kyle viewed her sardonically as she scrambled hastily to her feet. 'No rush. I can take a hint. Just don't put *too* much reliance on that manoeuvre.'

'I shan't need to,' she said, pulling the robe about her and tightening the belt in an effort to regain a little dignity. 'I'll make darn sure I don't get near enough again to precipitate another attack!'

'Of course you will.' The ambiguity of that statement was underlined by the mocking smile. 'Better get dressed. We don't want to be late.'

Shannon tossed the tumbled mass of blonde hair back over her shoulder in a gesture that smacked more of defiance than indifference as she turned away. 'We can hardly avoid it. It's nearly half past two now.'

'In which case, we'd both better hurry.'

She hastened her steps as he threw back the sheet and slid out of the bed, resisting the urge to glance back at him. She didn't need to see him to know he was aroused; she had been close enough to have tangible proof.

Touching him that way had been foolish, to say the least, too reminiscent of times in the past when she had woken him from sleep to make love to her. He had never been loath then either. It was to his credit that he'd held fire just now, knowing full well that she was on the verge of being unable to say no. Many men would have gone ahead and taken advantage of that weakness.

If she wanted to emerge from this episode with pride at least intact, she had better take steps to curb her libido, she told herself wryly, closing the door of her own room. Once she gave into it, she was lost.

The home was situated on the north side of the rambling, evergreen city. A big old house with a canopied front entrance, it stood in its own grounds and looked well-maintained. A group of younger children were playing some game in the afternoon sunshine, while an older section tended the flowerbeds scattered about the spacious lawn fronting the house.

None of them looked the least bit miserable, Shannon was glad to see.

They were greeted by a cheerful lady in her mid-fifties who answered to the name of Mrs Robinson. She took the two of them into a sunny sitting room, empty at the moment but generally well-used if the rather shabby furnishings were anything to go by.

'The older children gather in here after the younger ones are in bed,' she said. 'They can please themselves how they spend their time.' Her eyes twinkled. 'Within reason. No telling what a mixed bunch of teenagers might get up to left to their own devices for too long.'

Kyle laughed. 'No telling what a mixed bunch any age might get up to!'

Obviously not yet old enough to be past appreciating an attractive male, she gave him a roguish smile. 'True enough.'

'Is Jodie all right?' asked Shannon, thinking it was high time she got in on the act. 'I mean, how is she coping with losing her father?'

The older woman sobered immediately, apparently well attuned to atmospheric vibes. 'Extremely well.' She hesitated, looking from face to face with an air of not quite knowing how to put what she wanted to say. 'I think you might find Jodie a bit of a shock. She may only be nine in years, but she's going on forty in experience.'

Serious himself now, Kyle said sharply, 'What kind of experience?'

'Too many kinds, I'm afraid. To put it bluntly, her father was a drunk who hadn't had a proper job in years. He lived on state hand-outs, with most of it going on drink and women, from what we can put together. Jodie had to learn to fend more or less for herself. Which she seems to have done quite adequately, I must say. The trouble is—'

She broke off, shaking her head. 'Best if you see for yourself. She should be here any minute. I sent one of the girls to find her.'

As if on cue, the door opened, revealing a small skinny girl dressed in mud-splattered jeans and a blue shirt that was torn at the sleeve seam as if someone or something had yanked at the material. Behind her hovered a fifteen-year-old wearing a martyred expression.

'Fightin' again!' she intoned. 'Had to drag her off that stupid Robby! You'd think he'd have learned to keep his big mouth shut by now!'

'I shut it for him,' declared her charge matter-of-factly. 'I gave him a fat lip!'

'She did too,' confirmed the older girl. 'Made him cry.'

'He's a crybaby,' came the deprecating comment from below. 'A big fat crybaby!'

'That's enough now!' said Mrs Robinson hastily. 'All right, Betty, I'll handle it from here.'

Jodie stayed where she was, a self-contained figure, dark hair cropped short about a finely boned face splattered with mud, presumably from the same source as that covering her jeans. Eyes the same colour as Kyle's appraised the seated group coolly, fastening on Kyle himself as the obvious choice.

'I suppose you're my uncle.'

Lips twitching, he inclined his head. 'I suppose I am. You look very much like your mother did at your age—mud and all.'

That roused a faint spark of interest. 'I don't remember my mother.'

'Well, no, you wouldn't,' he said. 'You'll just have to take my word for it. She was always getting into scrapes of one kind or another. Not,' he added, 'that I remember her punching any boy's lights out!'

The grin was fleeting. 'I bet she could have done, though!'

'Given enough provocation, maybe.' Kyle indicated Shannon. 'Meet your aunt.'

Contained again, Jodie directed an unblinking grey gaze at her. 'Hello.'

Shannon restrained an impulse to get up and go to the girl. Kyle had remained seated, probably so as not to tower over the diminutive figure. She did the same, smiling warmly. 'Hello, Jodie.'

It was Mrs Robinson who got to her feet. 'I'll leave the three of you to get acquainted,' she said. 'Come on in, Jodie. They've already seen you, so there's not much point in cleaning you up first. Just try not to get too much dirt on the cushion covers. They were only washed last week.'

To Kyle, she added, 'Take all the time you want. I'll get somebody to bring some tea in.'

'With buns?' asked Jodie, displaying another spark of interest.

'With buns,' agreed her benefactor drily.

Silence reigned for a few seconds after the door had closed behind the matron. Jodie had taken a few steps further into the room, but was standing once more as if rooted to the spot, face wiped clean of all expression. Not quite as unconcerned as she was making out, though, Shannon realised, noting the hands curled into small, tight fists at her sides.

This time she took the initiative, easing the neckline of her lemon cotton dress away from her skin with a grimace. 'I don't know about anyone else, but I'm hot! Are we allowed to open a window in here?'

Jodie shrugged thin shoulders. 'I guess. There isn't any air-conditioning.'

'I don't suppose funds run to it.' Kyle got up and went to the nearest window, opening both casements to admit a flow of scarcely cooler air. 'Nice place, all the same.'

'It's all right.' Jodie sounded less than enthusiastic. 'There's a lot of rules.'

'With so many people living here, I imagine there has to be,' said Shannon lightly. 'Anyway, you won't be here much longer. You're coming back to England with us.'

The curled fists showed no sign of relaxing. 'Am I?'

'Where else would you go?' Leaning against the windowsill, hands thrust comfortably into trouser pockets, Kyle both looked and sounded at ease. 'You're family. Families belong together.'

She digested that for a moment, obviously not wholly impressed. 'Dad didn't think so,' she observed at length. 'He said I was a liability.'

How could anyone do that to a child? wondered Shannon in swift seething anger. Uncharitable maybe to think ill of the dead, but from what she had heard so far the man had been somewhat short on redeeming features.

'You're no liability to us,' she said before Kyle could answer himself. 'We're looking forward to having you home with us.' Her voice gained in enthusiasm. 'You'll love Holly House, Jodie. There's a huge garden, with a pond and ducks. An orchard too. It will be a lot colder than it is here to start with, but there's spring and summer to come, and the weather's lovely then.' The last with crossed fingers. 'You'll have your own room, and lots of toys, and—'

'I'm too old for toys,' came the disdainful intervention.

'Lots of other things, then,' Shannon substituted, refusing to be thrown. 'There's a really good school not too far away. You'll...'

'Robby said I'd have to go to boarding-school.' If Jodie had perked up at all, she was back to unemotionalism again. 'He said all British kids have to go to boarding-school.'

'Just how old is this Robby?' asked Kyle.

The shrug came again. 'Don't know. About twelve, I suppose.'

Kyle turned a laugh into a cough. 'Small for his age, I take it?'

'No, he's big and fat.' This time there was a definite hint of impatience in her tone. 'I already told you that.'

'So you did. I thought you were speaking figuratively.' He shook his head as the slim dark brows drew together, forestalling the question obviously about to be asked. 'Whatever, he was wrong. Not all British kids go to boarding-school. I didn't. Neither did Shannon. You don't have to go. That's a promise.'

One he was going out on a limb to give, taking their situation into account, thought Shannon. If she had been staying on permanently herself it would have been a different matter. She liked to keep office hours when she was working on a book, which would fit in well enough with school, but once Kyle got started it was next to impossible to tear him away in mid-flow.

Not her worry, she reminded herself, and knew she was lying. Little lost Jodie had already got to her. Her own childhood had been idyllic, her parents the best in the world. How could she contemplate robbing this child of the one opportunity she had of becoming part of a real family?

Yet how could she contemplate staying with a man who felt nothing for her beyond a purely physical desire? She had already trodden that road. It would be suicidal to try it again.

She became suddenly aware of two pairs of eyes fastened on her, one set enigmatic as always, the other revealing a cynicism far beyond their owner's years.

'You don't really want me,' Jodie stated without rancour. 'You're just saying it.'

'That's not true!' Other problems temporarily sidelined, Shannon concentrated every ounce of her attention on the small dirty face in an effort to convince. 'Of course I want you! We both want you! Why else would we have come eleven thousand miles to find you?'

If an answer had been forthcoming, it was diverted by the rattle of teacups outside the door. 'Buns!' Jodie exclaimed, showing the first genuine enthusiasm of the day.

She went without being asked to open the door and admit the girl wheeling a small wooden trolley, counting the cakes set out ready on a plate as it was pushed across to where Shannon was seated. 'Six,' she announced. 'That's two each—unless you don't want any?' she added with a hopeful glance. 'Bet you're on a diet, aren't you? Dad's girlfriends are always on diets!'

'Not all women need to diet,' said Kyle before Shannon could come up with a response, obviously deeming it best to leave the rest of that statement alone. 'But I'm no bun-eater, so you can have mine.'

'Ma Robinson will skin you if you eat them all yourself,' said the trolley-pusher self-righteously.

'She won't know if you don't tell her,' was the prompt reply, accompanied by a glower. 'You do, and I'll put a spider in your bed. A big one!'

'I think you might be safer staying out of it,' advised Kyle, straight-faced, though only just.

'She wouldn't dare!' exclaimed the girl, but she didn't sound too sure. 'Anyway,' she added by way of a get-out, 'they're your buns.'

Jodie watched her back out of the room with a certain satisfaction before turning to the trolley to carefully select the biggest and most succulent-looking cake. 'I would too,' she said, biting into it with firm white teeth. 'I already did it to one of the others.'

Don't talk with your mouth full, it was on the tip of

Shannon's tongue to admonish, but she bit back the retort, lifting her shoulders in a philosophical little shrug as she caught Kyle's amused eye. If buns were what it took to turn Jodie into a reasonably normal nine-year-old, then let her get on with them. Manners could wait.

She poured the tea, and handed Kyle a cup, sipping her own while she watched his niece demolish all six cakes.

'Don't they feed you very well here?' she felt bound to ask.

'It's okay.' The last crumb went the way of the first, followed by a regretful sigh. 'Better than at home. Dad never got a lot of food in.'

'Do you miss him?' asked Kyle, mouth suddenly grim.

Jodie considered the question, her head on one side. 'Not much,' she acknowledged.

'You'll get plenty to eat from now on,' Shannon assured her, shuddering to think what kind of life she must have led. 'Plenty of everything! We're going to take you back to our hotel until everything is sorted out. We'll do some shopping. Just the two of us, if your uncle doesn't want to come.' She gave the girl a conspiratorial smile. 'Men aren't too keen on going round the shops.'

'I can always take off if the going gets too rough,' said Kyle drily, adding on a cautioning note, 'Though it might be an idea to get the go-ahead before you start making too many plans.'

Jodie looked from one to the other, expression thoughtful, as if weighing the two of them up. When she spoke again it was with a new purpose in her voice. 'I've never been in a hotel.'

'There's a whole lot of new things you're going to be experiencing!' Shannon was too enthused to heed Kyle's warning. 'I don't imagine you've ever flown before either?'

The grey eyes took on a sudden glint of mischief. 'I haven't got any wings.'

'I wouldn't put it past you to sprout them.' Kyle was smiling, though the glance he winged Shannon's way was somewhat lacking in humour. 'How about going and finding Mrs Robinson for us?'

'Okay.' There was no doubting the readiness. 'I know where she'll be.'

Shannon waited until the door had closed before saying ruefully, 'I know. I shouldn't have raised her expectations like that before talking to Mrs Robinson.'

'No, you shouldn't,' Kyle agreed hardily. 'We'll just have to hope that she goes along with it. Not that it might be up to her alone.' He viewed her for a moment, noting the concern in the green eyes, the tendrils of golden hair clinging damply to her temples, his expression softening a fraction. 'Still a creature of impulse!'

'With few of them for the best.' She made a helpless little gesture. 'It's all wrong, isn't it? We're here under false pretences!'

The tolerance vanished. 'So what was the alternative? Good as this place seems to be, it's still an institution. Jodie needs more than that; she deserves more than that. All right, so it's not going to be all that easy once you're out of the picture, but I'll manage.'

There would be no shortage of help from other sources, for sure, thought Shannon dispiritedly. He might even marry again once their divorce came through. Having met Jodie, she already hated the thought of anyone else taking over, but the only other course was still out of the question.

Mrs Robinson put in an appearance alone. 'I hear you

want to take Jodie back to the hotel with you?' she said without preamble.

It was Kyle who answered. 'If it's allowed, yes, we do. We realise there'll be formalities to complete before we take her out of the country, of course, but it would be better if we could spend whatever time it takes together.'

'For all concerned, I think,' agreed the woman with a hint of humour. 'I've just seen Robby's fat lip.'

'Then it's all right?' said Shannon in relief. 'That's great! How long do you think it might be before we can take her home?'

'I'd think you'd get everything fixed up on Monday. It's not like she's an Aussie. I sent her to get washed and changed, by the way. Not that you'll find it much of an improvement. All she had when she was brought in was a couple of pairs of pants and a few tops. We keep a stock of clothes for kids like Jodie to choose from, but she wouldn't even look at the dresses.'

Shannon laughed. 'I was a bit of a tomboy myself, but I grew out of it. I'm sure Jodie will too.'

'Plenty of time for it,' agreed the older woman. 'Have you got any children of your own?'

'No,' she acknowledged.

'Not yet,' Kyle appended smoothly.

'Good luck, then.' She turned as Jodie appeared in the open doorway behind her, shaking her head as she took in the cotton trousers and shirt that had once been a blue and white print but had now faded to an overall blur. 'Why did you put those old things on?'

'Because the other things aren't mine,' was the unfazed reply, drawing another exasperated shake of the head.

'Well, at least they're clean. Where's your bag?'

'In the hall.' Jodie switched her gaze to Kyle. 'Can we go now?'

'On our way,' he said.

The four of them arrived at the front door to find the long, low saloon Kyle had hired to drive them here surrounded by children. Flushed with self-importance, Jodie informed them all that she was going in the car to a hotel, then in a plane to England where she was going to be living in a big house with dozens of rooms and a duck pond in the garden.

She took her leave of Mrs Robinson with an obvious lack of regret, lifting a languid hand in farewell to the gathered children as the car drew away. Once out of sight of the house, she relaxed back into her seat, hand smoothing the soft leather.

'Nice car,' she commented. 'Is it yours?'

'Rented.' Kyle glanced at the small figure in the driving mirror, lips curving. 'You know a lot about cars?'

'Not like this one,' she said, taking the question at face value. 'Dad's was an old wreck. Have you got a car in England?'

'Two,' Shannon confirmed. 'Three, if you count mine.'

'Three cars!' There was a wealth of satisfaction in the young voice. 'I think I'm going to like it there.'

Soon after, not the least bit discomposed, on the surface at least, by the lush surroundings, she swanned through the hotel lobby and into the lift as if she had been doing it all her life.

'I'm going to live in England,' she announced to the other occupants. 'In a big house, with *three* cars!'

The suite drew approving sounds too. She went through it like a whirlwind, missing nothing on the way.

'Why are your things in one bedroom and Aunty Shannon's in the other?' she asked, coming back to the sitting room to eye the pair of them with disconcerting speculation. 'Did you have a row?' A trace of anxiety crossed her face when there was no immediate answer. 'Was it about me?'

'There wasn't any row,' Shannon hastened to assure her. 'We were tired after the journey, and didn't want to disturb one another, that's all.'

As explanations went, it was decidedly weak, but Jodie seemed to see no flaws in it, her face clearing again. 'I suppose you'll want the one with the big bed now, then,' she said. 'I'll carry your stuff through for you,' she added to Kyle.

She was gone again before either of them could reply. Kyle moved to block Shannon off as she made to follow her, his expression forceful.

'Leave it!'

Her mouth took on a firmer line of its own, belying the quivering reaction inside her. 'There's no way we're sharing a bed!'

'What else would you suggest?' he asked, voice low though no less cogent. 'You want to tell her the truth, after all you said to her back there? You want her to think you were lying through your teeth about how you felt?'

Shannon bit her lip. 'Of course I don't. And I wasn't. She's a terrific kid!'

'Yes, she is. She's also an emotionally damaged one. What she needs more than anything is a stable environment. What she *doesn't* need right now is to know we're not what we seem to be.'

'She'll have to know some time,' Shannon pointed out, and saw his eyes fire.

'You promised me three months.'

'Only so the adoption would go through. I didn't count on having to pretend…anything else.'

'There was no pretence about what you were feeling when you woke me this afternoon,' Kyle rejoined softly. 'None from my side either.' He reached out and drew her to him, taking no heed of her half-hearted resistance, hands cupping her face. 'Why don't we forget the rest for now, and just enjoy what's there? You know you want to.'

Looking deep into the grey eyes, heart hammering, her whole body quivering, Shannon felt an overwhelming urge to say, To hell with it. He was right. Why shouldn't they enjoy what they had? Three months was a long time.

But not infinite, came the rider. What about afterwards? What about Craig? If he was home, he would have read her letter by now. A purely platonic arrangement for the child's sake, she had told him. Was her word worth so little?

'I am *not* sleeping with you,' she said between her teeth. 'Get that through your head, will you? If we share a room, you sleep in a chair, or on the floor. Is that clear?'

Expecting anger, she was surprised, and not a little put out, when he simply laughed and let her go, eyes taunting. 'Your choice.'

Her loss, was what he meant, she thought, putting distance between them. He knew exactly how he made her feel. So far as he was concerned, there was no reason at all why they shouldn't indulge a mutual desire while they had the opportunity, because for him that was all it would mean. The danger on her side being that it would be all too easy to let her emotions become too deeply involved again.

A risk she wasn't prepared to take.

CHAPTER FIVE

JODIE'S return to the room was a relief. 'All done,' she announced, with a 'what now?' expression as she looked from one to the other.

'What would you like to do for the rest of the day?' asked Shannon, responding to the unspoken question. 'Your choice,' she added with deliberation, regretting it when she saw Kyle's grin from the corner of her eye.

'*Anything?*' asked Jodie hopefully.

'Within reason,' Kyle temporised. 'Still gives plenty of scope,' he added as the small face acquired a resigned look. 'Say what you have in mind, and we'll see.'

'Pizza first, then the cinema,' she said, resignation increasing as she watched his expression. 'I knew you wouldn't go for it!'

'It sounds fine to me,' Shannon put in before he could answer. 'Any particular film you fancy seeing?'

Jodie shook her head, eyes going back to Kyle in instinctive recognition that his was the ultimate word. 'It doesn't *have* to be pizza,' she conceded, obviously seeing that as the stumbling block. 'I like hamburgers too.'

'I'll take her myself if you don't fancy it,' said Shannon, resenting the deference. 'You can always have dinner here in the hotel.'

Kyle gave her a quelling glance. 'I didn't say I didn't fancy it. Should be an experience for us all. Pizza it is,' he told his niece, drawing a smile that dazzled. 'We'd better stop at the desk on the way and find out what's showing where.'

'I could do with taking a shower first,' Shannon protested. 'I'm all hot and sticky!'

'We don't have time.' His tone was unequivocal. 'Anyway, you'll be the same again as soon as you get outside.'

Shannon gave in. It was either that or be left behind herself. In this mood, Kyle was not open to argument, she knew of old.

It turned out to be an enjoyable enough evening all round. From the pizza parlour, they went on to see the latest science fiction film. Jodie's choice once again, but one Kyle heartily concurred with as a lover of the genre himself.

It wasn't to Shannon's particular taste, but she sat through it uncomplainingly while the two of them revelled in the special effects. There was a rapport developing between uncle and niece already. One she envied, if she was honest. The Beaumont blood ran through both sets of veins; it was she who was the outsider.

Fight it though she tried, it was obvious that Jodie was almost out on her feet by the time they got back to the hotel. She made no demur when Kyle despatched her straight off to bed on reaching the suite, pausing only to ask if they could visit Sea World the next day.

'There's one young lady who's going to have no trouble at all adjusting to a new life,' Kyle observed drily. 'I'd say we're going to have our work cut out catching up on everything she wants to do!'

Shannon sank into a chair, kicking off her sandals unthinkingly to curl her feet beneath her the way she usually did at home. The air-conditioning was a welcome relief from the humidity outside, though she refused to let her limp hair and moist skin bother her. The last thing she wanted was for Kyle to think she cared how she looked to him.

'She's worth the effort,' she said. 'Nine years old and that was her first visit to a cinema!'

'First authorised visit,' Kyle corrected. 'She told me a group of local kids would pool whatever they had to get one of them inside whenever they could, then he or she would open a fire door and let the rest sneak in during the film, while it was dark.'

Aware of a pang that could only be identified as jealousy, Shannon made an effort to sound light and easy. 'When did she tell you that?'

'We had quite a chat when you went to the Ladies.' By no means oblivious to the vibes, he added levelly, 'She hasn't had much reason up to now to put any trust in women.'

'I'd have thought she didn't have all that much reason to put her trust in a man, with her father for an example,' Shannon answered shortly.

'I didn't say she'd put her trust in me, simply that she'd talked to me,' Kyle returned on a mild note. 'It's going to take time to convince her that we're not going to get fed up and dump her. That's why she's making hay while the sun still shines.'

He went over to the built-in bar, squatting to open the door and survey the stock of bottles. 'Like a drink?'

The overhead light glinted in the thick dark hair, showing up the crisp line at his nape, the taut stretch of the white cotton-knit shirt across broad shoulders, and equally taut trouser seat. Anything, Shannon thought, swallowing on the ache in her throat, to put off the moment of retirement. Even if he kept his distance, sharing a room with him was going to be far from restful. If he didn't...

She cut off that train of thought abruptly. 'I'll have a screwdriver, if there's any orange juice.'

A lesser man might have pointed out that she could

scarcely have one if there wasn't, but Kyle wasn't one to waste his breath on pedantry. He mixed the same drink for them both, bringing them across to where she sat, and taking the other easy chair.

'Cheers,' he said briefly.

Shannon hadn't really wanted the drink. She put the glass down after the first sip, searching her mind desperately for something to say.

'Do you think we really might get it all sorted on Monday?' she asked at length.

'Can't see any reason why not,' he returned. 'As Mrs Robinson said, it isn't as if Jodie is an Australian national. I got a temporary passport issued for her, so there shouldn't be any problem at our end.'

'So we might be able to leave Tuesday?'

'Provided we could get a flight at short notice. We might have to wait a few days.'

A few days meant a few nights—a prospect Shannon didn't care to contemplate. 'I'll have to let Craig know what's happening,' she said with deliberation. 'I might try giving him a ring tomorrow.'

'Don't forget the time difference,' was all the comment she got.

There was another silence. This time Kyle was the one to break it, tossing back the rest of his drink to announce flatly, 'I'm ready for bed. Do I go first, or do you?'

Shannon avoided his gaze. Whichever way they handled it, it was going to be awkward, but at least if she went first she could make sure *she* secured the bed. 'I will,' she said. 'Give me fifteen minutes. I want that shower.'

'You've got ten,' he declared. 'I need a shower too.'

And he wouldn't be hanging fire if she wasn't out by the time he'd given her, she deduced. She got swiftly to her feet, leaving the almost untouched drink where it stood. There was no way she was giving him the excuse!

She was out of the shower within five minutes, and safely between sheets by the time he came through, her unwashed hair brushed through with cologne to freshen it. He didn't give her so much as a glance, just began stripping off his clothing.

Shannon turned on her side away from him as he unbuckled his belt. He was doing it on purpose, of course; he knew how easily he could turn her on. It was happening too, heat spiralling through her at the rasp of a zip, the double thud as shoes were shed, the sliding sound of cloth against flesh. She hardly dared draw breath until the bathroom door finally closed on him, afraid of giving herself away.

Having limited her to a few minutes, he spent a good twelve himself under the hot gush. Lying there listening, she could see him in her mind's eye, tanned body glistening with water, the musculature of arms and chest and thigh clearly defined. They had made love more than once in the shower. She could feel the urgency mounting inside her at the very memory.

Cut it out! she told herself desperately, but it made no difference.

What bedding she had been able to find was piled on one of the two chairs, but he ignored it when he eventually came through, coming straight over to the bed. Shannon forced herself to roll over to face him, taking in the blue pyjama bottoms with mingled emotions before lifting a fierce green gaze to meet sardonic grey.

'I already told you—'

'I've no intention of sleeping on the floor,' he said. 'If you don't like sharing the bed, you know what to do.'

He switched off the bedside lamp and got in, relaxing

onto his back with three feet of space between them. 'Goodnight.'

Shannon couldn't bring herself to answer. What she had wanted him to do, she admitted numbly, was to disregard what she had said—to take hold of her and *make* her respond to him. There had been a time when he would have done exactly that, but obviously not any more. He just didn't care enough.

It was snowing when they landed at seven on Saturday morning, though not heavily enough to cause any problems. Driving away from the airport, Jodie had her nose pressed against the window in pure rapture, watching the flakes swirl by.

'Just like in the movies!' she said, having picked up more than one Americanism from that source. 'Will I be able to build a snowman when we get to Holly House?'

'Depends whether it settles long enough.' Shannon stifled a yawn. 'The first thing we're all going to need is a good long sleep in a proper bed!'

'I'm not tired,' claimed the girl, belying that statement barely half a minute later by falling asleep.

'I could do with getting some things from the flat before we go to the house,' Shannon suggested tentatively as they turned onto the A4. 'I know it means a detour, but it would save coming all the way back again for a while.'

'You left a load of stuff at the house,' Kyle responded, not taking his eyes from the traffic-congested road ahead. 'Enough to be going on with, at any rate.'

A matter of opinion, she thought, but it wasn't worth arguing about. 'I'm surprised you didn't throw it all out,' she parried.

'I didn't see any reason.' He slid the car smoothly into line for the M25 junction, profile austere in the grey morning light. 'I had it all shifted into one of the spare bedrooms.'

'By whom?' she demanded tautly. 'Paula?'

This time he did give her a fleeting glance, seeing the glitter in the green eyes. 'What difference does it make?'

Plenty! she could have answered. The thought of that woman handling her things was enough to make her blood boil. 'I'd hardly expect you to understand,' she said instead. 'I'll bet you moved her in the same night I left!'

'Then you lose.' His tone was level. 'She was never in the house even one night.'

Shannon blocked out her weaker tendencies, voice heavy with irony. 'Am I expected to believe the same of the flat too?'

'Please yourself,' he said. 'You usually do.'

'If I'm so thoroughly self-centred, what am I doing here to start with?' she flung at him, stung by the accusation.

'I said usually, not thoroughly,' came the unmoved return. 'And keep your voice down.'

'Or else what?' It was an infantile retort, and she knew it, but she was too worked up to care.

'Or else you'll wake Jodie up,' he said, still in the same impassive tones.

Her fury died as swiftly as it had arisen, leaving her feeling anything but proud of herself. She was twenty-five, not twelve, for heaven's sake!

She turned to look at the sleeping child, her mood mellowing. She had formed a very real affection for her over the time they had been forced to wait for a flight home, and liked to believe that the feeling was in some part returned. Not that she stood a chance of competing with Kyle, of course. Right from the first there had been a special bond between them. Understandable, she supposed, when he had been so close to the sister Jodie resembled in so many ways.

The past few days had flown by; it was the nights that had dragged. She and Kyle had continued to share a bed, but there had been no attempt on his part to take it any further. She doubted that he would have said no if she'd made the approach herself, but no way had she been going to give him *that* satisfaction!

So far, they hadn't discussed sleeping arrangements at the house. The bedroom they had shared during their all-too-brief marital harmony had a dressing room adjoining, complete with convertible sofa divan. If Kyle refused to use it, she would take it herself, she thought resolutely now. That would at least keep up the façade in Jodie's eyes.

The snow lay deeper out around Tonbridge, although the present fall had all but petered out.

'Jodie's going to need some proper winter clothes,' Shannon observed as they turned into the wide gravelled driveway at last. 'The things I got her in Brisbane are hardly adequate.'

'You can take her into Tonbridge on Monday and fix her up,' Kyle responded. 'She's going to need school uniform too.'

'Wouldn't it be a good idea to make sure the school will take her first?' she asked, and saw his lips slant.

'Obviously.'

Meaning he'd already done it, which she should have known, of course. Where Jodie was concerned, nothing was to be left to chance.

She was silent as the car came to a stop in front of the lovely old house with its mullioned windows and imposing double oak doors, remembering the very first time she had seen it—the immediate conviction that this was the place they were going to buy. The house had been their main base, though the London apartment had seen plenty of action too. In those first months, life had been wonderful all round.

She blinked rapidly to clear the fine mist that had formed over her eyes, reluctant to have Kyle see her moved to tears over all they'd lost. All *she* had lost, at least, she amended. He had suffered no deprivation, for certain!

Jodie stirred when he switched the engine off, rubbing her eyes with the back of her fists as she came slowly and reluctantly back to consciousness.

'We're here,' Shannon told her, engendering a sudden animation.

The trousers and jacket Jodie was wearing were too thin for the outside temperature, especially for someone accustomed to a subtropical climate, but she was far from noticing any chill as she scrambled from the car to gaze wide-eyed at the building before her.

'It's nearly as big as the home!' she exclaimed, too impressed to remember the blasé act for a brief moment. She made a fast adjustment, causing Kyle to stifle a laugh as she added condescendingly, 'Not bad.'

There had been no changes made since she had left, Shannon was relieved to see on entering the panelled hall. The grandfather clock she had loved so much still ticked steadily away, the oak chest they had found in a local antiques shop still stood in the far corner, the pictures and other bits and pieces occupying the same positions she had chosen for them. If the rest of the house was untouched too, it would be almost as if she had never been away.

Jodie launched herself into exploration, disappearing up the wide branching staircase at a speed only the very young could attain. Bringing in the bags, Kyle dumped them unceremoniously on the floor, lifting an interrogative eyebrow at Shannon, who had made no move to go any further.

'No need to stand on ceremony,' he said. 'It's still as much your home as mine. Mrs Parkin will have got in enough to see us over the weekend, so we don't have to worry about food. We'll eat out later.'

'What about now?' she asked, making an effort to dissemble. 'I could cook you some breakfast.'

The dark brow flicked upwards again. 'Complete with blackened bacon and broken eggs still?'

Her smile was fleeting. 'A risk you'd have to take.'

'What's life without a little risk?' The grey eyes acquired a deeper hue as he studied her, noting the pallor of her face within the heavy frame of blonde hair. 'Shannon—'

Whatever he had been about to say was interrupted by a shout from the right-hand gallery above.

'Which room is going to be mine?'

'Second door along,' Kyle called back. 'And no bouncing on the bed! You nearly fetched the ceiling down at the hotel!'

The only answer was a giggle, reassuring in itself considering the lack of laughter in her young life prior to this.

Kyle was laughing too, the gaze he brought back to Shannon devoid now of its previous intensity. '*I'll* cook breakfast. You can make the coffee.'

He shed his light camel overcoat as he made for the kitchen, tossing it carelessly over a chair in passing. The fine needlecord trousers and lemon sweater looked good on his lean, powerful frame.

'Travel casual, travel in comfort,' he had said when they were dressing for the honeymoon flight to Bali—a maxim Shannon had followed herself since, as now, in her easy-fitting brown trousers and pale suede jacket.

Smart casual, of course. They were neither of them given to anything other.

For a moment back there he had seemed on the verge of saying something important, she mused, flinging her jacket over his as she followed at a slower pace. Not that she imagined it would have been what she would most like to hear from him.

Given the time over again, she would handle things so differently. What he'd wanted was a wife capable of acting like an adult woman; what she'd given him was a capricious brat constantly trying him out. She was doing it still to a certain extent, she supposed. Only he wasn't rising to it any more. Not in any sense, it seemed.

Jodie came tumbling back down the stairs, face alight. 'It's fab!' she declared, forsaking the blasé act for good and all. 'Everything is simply fab! Can I go outside?'

'You don't have any suitable shoes or clothes yet,' Shannon reminded her, wondering how they were going to get through the whole weekend without. 'I'll tell you what,' she added, dismissing all thoughts of bed for the present, 'as soon as we've had breakfast, we'll take the car and go shopping. The snow will still be here when we get back.'

'It will probably be here for several days, if the forecast is anything to go by,' said Kyle, catching the last as they entered the warm farmhouse-style kitchen, where he had switched on the radio. 'There's a high pressure on the way. That means heavy frosts this time of year.'

He took a pack of bacon from the refrigerator and sliced it open, laying all eight rashers across the waiting grid, and sliding it beneath the already reddening grill. Jodie watched him slice tomatoes with the same efficiency, followed by mushrooms.

'Don't you like cooking?' she asked Shannon, who was making the coffee.

'Not much,' Shannon admitted. 'Probably because I'm not much good at it.'

'None of Dad's girlfriends were either,' was the matter-of-fact response. 'Dad said they were all of them only good for one thing.'

Shannon saw Kyle's mouth go taut, the knuckles of the hand wielding the knife whiten. She waited with bated breath for Jodie to enlarge on the statement, but she said no more, wandering off to finish exploring the ground floor until breakfast was ready.

'If that brother-in-law of mine was still alive, I'd kill him myself!' Kyle exclaimed grimly.

'If he was still alive, Jodie wouldn't be here anyway,' Shannon pointed out. 'At least she's out of it now. By this time next year she'll probably have forgotten most of it.'

'And where will *you* be this time next year?' he asked in the same hard tones.

Where she would like to be was right here, but she wasn't about to admit it. 'I don't know,' she said, voice as steady as she could make it. 'I suppose it depends on how long it takes for the divorce to come through.'

'I dare say Craig will hold out for you.'

An ungovernable desire to cut him down gave her tongue an acid edge. 'Longer than you ever could, for sure!'

She regretted the crack the moment the words were out of her mouth, biting her lip as she viewed his expressionless face. 'Kyle, I didn't...'

This time it was Jodie's appearance in the doorway that caused the rest to be left unsaid. The pixie features took on a sudden disquieting expectancy as she looked from one to the other, obviously sensing the atmosphere. 'Are you going to fight?' she asked.

Shannon summoned a smile. 'Of course not! We were just talking, that's all.'

'Don't lie to her,' Kyle said sharply, adding on a quieter note, 'Adults sometimes get angry with each other for very little reason, Jodie.'

'I know.' She sounded as if it was only natural. 'Dad had rows all the time.'

'Well, we shan't be doing that,' he assured her. 'Shall we?' he said, with a meaningful glance in Shannon's direction.

'No,' she agreed, mentally crossing her fingers. 'It was strictly a one-off.' She lightened her tone. 'How about helping me lay the table?'

Jodie's appetite was more than equal to the plateful Kyle put before her some minutes later, Shannon's nowhere near her own portion—especially feeling the way she did feel. She stole a glance at him as he took his place at the table, trying to guess what he was thinking—without success, as usual. He was a master of the impassive expression.

Nasty as the crack she had made had been, he'd hardly have taken it to heart. He knew his own capabilities. Never once in all the times he had made love to her had he left her unsatisfied.

Her inner thigh muscles went into sudden, involuntary spasm, sending a ripple effect through her body. She put out the tip of her tongue to dampen lips gone dry, desisting abruptly as she met the grey eyes full-on. That he knew exactly what *she* was thinking right now was only too obvious.

'Are you coming shopping too, Uncle Kyle?' asked Jodie, apparently oblivious to any undercurrents.

'Knowing how women shop, I think I'd better,' he said. 'You'll need someone to help carry it all.'

She eyed him consideringly, eyes bright. 'You must have *lots* of money!'

He laughed. 'I might not have if I don't get back to work pretty soon.'

Shannon pricked her ears, professional interest taking precedence over other concerns for the moment. 'Do you have a book on the go?'

'More than halfway through,' he acknowledged. 'I changed my routine after you left. Oddly enough, some of the action takes place in Australia. I was out there only a few months ago researching background detail.' He glanced at his niece, whose attention had been drawn now to the window, where snow could be seen falling again, dropping his voice. 'I'm only sorry I didn't make more of an effort then.'

'I shouldn't have thought there was much you could have done at the time, anyway,' Shannon commented. 'Apart from maybe getting yourself charged with GBH.'

'No maybe about it.' He lightened his expression, the familiar mockery playing about his mouth as he regarded her. 'You're not eating.'

'I'm not hungry,' she countered. 'Sorry.'

His shrug was dismissive. 'An eleven-hour time difference can take some adjusting to. You'll feel better after a good night's sleep.'

There were other ways in which she could be made to feel better still, came the treacherous thought, and she hastily dropped her gaze. When it came to mind over matter, the contest was fast getting out of hand.

It was Kyle who suggested that she find a warm woolly of some kind to go under Jodie's jacket until she was fitted with a proper winter coat. About to ask the girl if she wanted to come and help her find something suitable, Shannon remembered just in time that she didn't even know in which of the spare rooms her things were stored at present.

Keeping the child in the dark regarding the true state of affairs was becoming increasingly difficult, she thought wryly on her way upstairs. In fact, the whole idea was lousy! No man living on his own would be allowed official custody of a nine-year-old girl who wasn't his own child, Kyle had said. So what if it was discovered that the two of them had parted right after the adoption had been formalised? Wasn't it possible that Jodie might be taken away again?

No use trying to tell herself it wasn't her problem. It had become as much her concern as Kyle's the moment she'd agreed to the arrangement. How was she going to feel if Jodie finished up in a home after all?

Guilty as hell, was the only possible answer, but she still couldn't contemplate the solution.

She found the clothes she had left behind stored in one of the unused bedrooms. There were more of them than she had imagined, but then, her wardrobe had been the last thing on her mind the day she'd walked out.

The dark red trouser suit would do, she decided, pulling out a white roll-necked sweater to go with it. For Jodie, she found a blue top that had been one of her own favourites. It was going to be big on the child, of course, but at least it would be warm. It was only temporary anyway.

She had a quick shower in the guest bathroom, and got into clean underwear. Back in the bedroom, she donned the red trousers and sweater, along with a pair of black ankle boots, turning to view herself in the cheval-glass as she fastened the three-quarter-length jacket. Apart from her hair, which was a few inches shorter, and a subtle difference about the eyes, she might have gone back in time. If only, she thought ruefully, it really was possible to turn back the clock!

She hadn't heard Kyle come upstairs, but he emerged from the master bedroom as she came along the landing. Wearing a sheepskin jacket now, he looked big and powerful and...dangerous.

'I always did like you in that suit,' he commented. 'But then, you look good in anything.'

Out of anything, too, the glint in his eyes suggested.

He indicated for her to go first, following too close for comfort. Shannon controlled the urge to hurry her steps. If she stumbled he would catch her, and she didn't want him touching her. Not with every nerve-ending already over-sensitised.

Jodie donned the blue top without argument, fingers stroking the soft mohair. 'It feels lovely,' she said. 'Can I have one like this?'

'You can have several,' Shannon promised her extravagantly. 'Of everything! We'll start from the skin and work out.'

'No frilly frocks, though,' the girl said on a definite note. 'I'm not wearing frilly frocks!'

'I don't think they'd suit you anyway,' said Kyle. 'Far too young.'

Jodie looked gratified. 'That's what I told Ma Robinson, but *she* said I was just being silly! I like pants best.'

'Me too.' Kyle returned the grin. 'All the same, I reckon a bit of compromise might be called for.'

With regard to school uniform, almost certainly, Shannon thought, wondering when Kyle was going to bring the subject up. It was his concern anyway.

She didn't get much of a look-in between the two of them at all when it came down to it. Jodie had very firm ideas on what she did and didn't like, and for the most part was allowed her own way. Shannon managed to sneak in no more than a couple of skirts and blouses, and those the least fancy available.

Kyle didn't see school uniform as a particularly urgent priority, she gathered when he finally suggested they head for home. Which was probably for the best. Jodie had enough new experiences to cope with at present.

It was when they were making their way back to the car park that they ran into the last person she would have wanted to meet—the last person she would have expected to meet here in Tonbridge.

Wearing a full-length mink coat, in typical defiance of present-day attitudes, dark hair tucked under a matching, wide-brimmed hat, Paula was even better-looking than she remembered from the one time she had actually laid eyes on the woman, her face a smooth oval, dark brows delicately arched above eyes the colour of old topaz. Her mouth was the only marring feature: mercenary was the word that sprang most readily to mind.

Whatever the other woman's true feelings on seeing the three of them together, they were kept well-concealed. Her smile was smooth.

'Quite a family picture!' she remarked.

Kyle inclined his head, revealing little himself. 'Jodie's my niece. You're looking well, Paula.'

'I'm doing *very* well,' she returned with subtle emphasis. The topaz gaze switched to Shannon, acquiring a colder light in the process. 'Better luck this time.'

Determined not to let the animosity raging inside her show through, Shannon returned her gaze unflinchingly. 'Thanks. You too.'

The laugh was barbed. '*I* never needed to rely on luck.' She looked back at Kyle, lingering for a deliberated moment before lifting a languid hand in farewell and continuing on her way.

Jodie was the first to break the small silence as the three of them moved on. 'I didn't like *her*,' she said with a positiveness that warmed Shannon's heart.

'Me neither,' she confirmed, seeing no reason to put on an act for Kyle's benefit. 'She's a bitch!'

The grin was pure devilment. 'Dad would have called her a bloody bitch!'

'That's enough!' Kyle's tone cut like a knife. 'Both of you!'

Shannon was bound to concede the point, though she was the one at fault for using the word in the first place. Jodie had simply been repeating what she had heard.

'It was wrong of me to say that,' she told the momentarily sobered child. 'Wrong of your father too. It isn't a nice thing to say about anybody.'

True, though, she tagged on mentally. Paula Frearson *was* an out-and-out bitch to do what she had done! The fact that Kyle had known her before his marriage had somehow made the betrayal even worse. She risked a glance at him, registering the grim expression. The affair had been terminated by mutual agreement some time ago, he had intimated, but from the way he'd jumped on the two of them for daring to pull her down, he obviously still felt something for her. Was it possible that Paula herself had been the one to lose interest once the challenge of a wife had been removed?

And, in which case, wasn't it also possible that with said wife back *in situ,* the interest might be renewed?

CHAPTER SIX

Resilient by nature, Jodie had recovered her spirits by the time they reached the car, eager to get back to the house and don the clothing that would enable her to spend the rest of the afternoon in the snow. What she couldn't do was keep the Sandman at bay. Before they'd gone half a mile she was fast asleep again.

'Next time you feel a need to express yourself, just make sure she isn't in the vicinity,' Kyle said tautly. 'She heard enough terminology from her father without you adding to it!'

'I already admitted I was wrong to say it,' Shannon responded, equally tautly. 'Not that it changes my opinion any.'

He swung the wheel to take a right-hand turn, pulling into the line of traffic leaving the town, his glance lacking in tolerance. 'It's all in the past. Let's leave it there, shall we?'

She let it go, turning her mind resolutely to other matters. One thing she must do today was ring Craig. She had found various excuses for not phoning him from Brisbane, but she could hardly go on avoiding the issue. He obviously wasn't going to like the arrangement, but he would surely appreciate the position she was in?

Her parents would be waiting for a call too. True to form, her mother had viewed the whole thing as an opportunity for a brand new start. Shannon hadn't had the heart to disillusion her, although it was going to be so much harder when the time came.

Jodie woke up when they reached the house. Ten

minutes later, dressed in the snazzy trousers and quilted jacket that had been her very first choice, she was off into the garden with strict instructions to stay away from the iced-over pond.

Pausing only to shed his coat, Kyle had gone straight to the study. When he closed the door as he had, it meant he didn't want to be disturbed for anything less than an emergency. Whether he intended writing, or simply wanted to be out of her way for a while, Shannon refused to care. Right now, she had other concerns.

Overlooking the rear of the house, the morning room had always been her favourite. Even today, with the sky grey and heavy and darkness not too far away, the off-white sofas and pastel-blue walls brought light into the room. She took a seat to dial the familiar number with a reluctance she had to fight to overcome.

Craig answered almost immediately, his tone leaving no doubt at all of his feelings. 'Where on earth have you been all week?' he demanded.

Shannon felt her heart sink. 'You didn't get my letter?'

'No, I didn't.' He sounded puzzled now. 'When did you send it?'

'Last week.' She aimed a mental imprecation at the post office, hardly knowing how or where to start explaining the situation. 'There's something I have to tell you,' she said slowly. 'Only it's difficult.'

The pause was lengthy. When Craig spoke again, his voice was heavier. 'You want to finish things between us; is that it?'

'It isn't that,' she hastened to assure him, deaf to the little voice at the back of her mind. 'It's like this...'

She did her best to give a lucid account, sensing his growing disapprobation. 'It's only until the adoption is finalised,' she ended. 'We can still see one another between times.'

'With you in Kent and me here in town?' he said shortly. 'That husband of yours should be shot for dragging you into this! It's criminal deception!'

'There's no crime in his wanting to look after his sister's child,' Shannon defended. 'You'd surely feel the same in his shoes?'

'I think she'd be better off all round being placed with a foster family,' he declared. 'How can a man his age have any idea how to cope with a child on his own—especially a girl?'

More or less what she had thought herself at first, Shannon was bound to admit. Still did to a great extent, though she wasn't prepared to say it aloud.

'He can scarcely make a worse job of it than her father was doing,' she said instead. 'And I'm sure he'll have no difficulty finding someone to help when he needs advice. All he needs me for is—'

'To circumvent the law,' Craig finished, which wasn't the way she had been going to put it but was true enough, she supposed.

'I can't do anything else,' she pleaded. 'She's all that's left of his sister, and he's all Jodie has left in the world!' She hesitated as an idea occurred to her, added tentatively, 'Craig, you wouldn't...inform anybody, would you?'

'Meaning the authorities?' His voice had cooled. 'You see me capable of that?'

'No. I mean, I just thought—' She broke off, running a distracted hand through her hair. 'I'm sorry. Of course you wouldn't. I know it's a lot to ask, but—'

'It is,' he said. 'A hell of a lot!' There was another pause, a long-drawn-out sigh. 'You know how I feel about you, Shannon. I can hardly pretend to like the idea of you moving back in with your husband.'

'It's a big house,' she returned. 'We'll hardly be on top of one another.' Not exactly a good choice of phrase, came the thought. 'Different rooms, separate lives,' she hastened to add. 'Trust me, Craig.'

'I do,' he said. 'It's him I don't trust. Having you there—'

'He isn't *having* me anywhere,' she stated flatly, once again tuning out the faint voice. 'You can be assured of that. This is strictly for Jodie.'

The sigh came again. 'All right. But only on condition that we see each other at least once a week between times. You can get up to town, can you?'

If the alternative was meeting him locally, then the answer had to be yes, Shannon reflected. Kyle would just have to manage on his own for a few hours. Good practice for him, anyway.

'Of course,' she agreed. 'You name the day and I'll fit in.'

They arranged to meet for lunch on Wednesday. Ringing off, Shannon drew a long, steadying breath, feeling the strain of the last few minutes. This was only the beginning. It wasn't going to get any easier.

Kyle emerged from the study at six, to find the two other members of the household sharing a sofa in the morning room and watching a game show on television.

'The woman there just won a car!' exclaimed his niece enthusiastically. 'And a whole lot of other things as well!'

'Must be her lucky day,' he commented on a dry note. 'Enjoy the snow, did you?'

'Oh, yes, great! I'm going to build a snowman to-morrow. You can help, if you like,' she add-ed generously.

The smile was genuine. 'I'll look forward to that. It's been a long time since I had an excuse.'

He took a seat in a nearby chair, lifting one leg over the other in an easy posture that gave Shannon a nostalgic reminder of past evenings when they had relaxed together. Not that there had been very many relaxing evenings, she had to admit.

Things were different these days; *she* was different. Growing up, it was called.

'Mrs Parkin left a casserole in the fridge, if you don't feel like going anywhere,' she said diffidently. 'I could put it on to reheat in the microwave. Even I can't make a mess of that!'

'*I* can cook,' announced Jodie. 'Some things, anyway,' she added, apparently deciding to err on the side of caution. 'I'll show you, if you like.'

'Thanks.' Shannon was cautious herself, not wanting to hurt the child's feelings. 'Maybe another day.'

'The casserole sounds a good idea,' Kyle agreed. 'I think we could all do with an early night.' He met the green eyes flicked sharply his way, face expressionless. 'We've hardly slept in two days.'

'*I* have,' Jodie claimed. 'I'll stay up and watch television.'

'You'll go to bed when you're told to go to bed, young lady,' he returned with mock severity, and received a cheeky grin.

'Worth a try.'

Listening to the exchange, Shannon had to laugh. Many children living the kind of life Jodie must have led would have finished up seriously disturbed, but not this one. Her spirit was indefatigable.

'I'll put the casserole in,' she said, getting up. 'You two enjoy the rest of the show.'

She had to pass by Kyle's chair on the way to the

door. Head back against the rest, he gave her a lazy scrutiny.

'Like old times,' he murmured.

'Like hell!' she retorted *sotto voce*.

His mouth widened briefly. 'We'll see.'

She contented herself with a scornful look, knowing she didn't deceive him for a second. Shirt-sleeves rolled to reveal muscular forearms and supple wrists, he stirred her senses the way he always had. Even suspecting what she did, if he'd reached out right then and pulled her down to him, she would have found it difficult to resist him.

Not that it was likely with Jodie in the room, of course. The child was her safeguard—against herself as much as him.

Heated through, the casserole went down well enough, the bottle of wine Kyle opened to go with it even better. Jodie was allowed a small glass, much to her approval. She'd only ever had beer before this, she advised with devastating factualism. Wine was much nicer.

Despite her claim, she was yawning her head off by eight o'clock and went off quite willingly to bed, declining with disdain Shannon's semi-joking offer to come up and tuck her in.

Kyle showed little inclination to start a conversational ball rolling after the child had departed. He had put a match to the log fire already laid in the sitting room, and was seemingly content to sit there before it, whisky glass to hand.

There had been times in the beginning when they had made love by firelight. Shannon could visualise the scene now: the thick cream rug spread with cushions, flame-bronzed limbs entwined, Kyle's face above her, eyes smouldering, the driving force of his loins.

Only a marriage couldn't be sustained on sex alone,

however good it might be. She'd been too young for him in more ways than just years. Fantasising about excitingly dominant men was one thing, actually living with one quite another. She hadn't known how to handle him.

Not that she could claim to be any nearer now.

'When do you plan on talking to Jodie about school?' she asked, desperate to break the silence.

His shrug was easy. 'We'll give her a few days to get used to being here before throwing her in at the deep end. It's bound to be a bit traumatic, even for her—especially if she's assessed at a lower grade than her year.'

'You think there's a chance she might be?'

'A good one, I'd say. She's street-wise, which indicates a lot of time spent *on* the streets rather than in school. They'll sort her out at Silverwood.'

Shannon hesitated before giving voice to her doubts. 'Considering what happened to Robby, do you think she's going to fit in at a school like Silverwood?'

The grey eyes regarded her dispassionately. 'What you really mean is she'd be more at home in a rougher environment.'

'Not all state-run schools are rough environments,' Shannon disputed. 'The local one certainly doesn't seem to be.'

'Maybe not, but she's still going to Silverwood.' Kyle shook his head as she made to say something else. 'It isn't open to discussion.'

Resentment flared in her, striking amber sparks in her eyes. 'Don't come the heavy with me! You still need my help, remember?'

'Which you're not going to withdraw because it isn't in your nature to go back on your word.'

For all the impact her anger was having on him, she

might as well have stayed mum, but that wasn't in her nature either. 'There's a first time for everything!'

'Not in this instance.' He paused, viewing the cascade of golden hair and enticingly fire-lit face, expression subtly altering. 'Same sleeping arrangements as before, I take it?'

Caught unawares by the sudden change of subject, Shannon took a firm grip on her wayward emotions. 'Not quite. You'll be using the dressing-room bed.'

His laugh was derisive. 'Not on your life! I like my own bed.'

'All right,' she parried, 'so *I'll* sleep in the dressing room.'

The derision increased. 'Fine. You do that.'

Silence fell again, disturbing Kyle not the slightest. Shannon had a strong inclination to throw something heavy at him, if only to disrupt that equanimity for a moment or two. The only thing stopping her was the suspicion that she was the one likely to be disrupted if she did.

'So what exactly is the procedure for the adoption?' she asked at length, adding with deliberation, 'I assume you've already put the wheels in motion?'

The cliché drew a faint grin. 'I contacted the appropriate people, yes. The major checks will probably have been done already. Next thing should be a visit from a social worker to view the house and judge whether we're likely to prove adequate parents. That's where you come in.'

'Supposing they've found out that we're separated?'

'No reason why they should. It was never official. So far as the records go, we've been married nearly three years. All we have to be is convincing.'

'An idyllically happy couple!' She snapped her fingers. 'All the way!'

His lips thinned, humour wiped away. 'It would be like you to overplay it just for kicks!'

'That's unfair!' she protested, already regretting the flippancy. 'I'm hardly going to risk ruining things for Jodie just to get at *you*!'

'So cut out the satire,' he said. 'Try acting like an adult for once!'

Several cutting rejoinders jostled for position on her tongue, rejected because none of them adequately expressed her feelings. She was on the losing end anyway. This was no time for immature retaliation.

'I'll play the part,' she assured him shortly. 'It won't be my fault if we fail to convince.'

The grey eyes roved her face, losing nothing of their steeliness in the process. 'It had better not be.'

Shannon let that pass too, angry as it made her. She was giving three months of her life to this project. Wasn't that enough?

She eyed him with concentrated loathing as he relaxed back into the chair—knowing it was all a front. Whatever she might suspect him of, he still aroused the same overriding desire in her. Her body yearned for his touch, for the feel of his lips, his muscular strength. That she could have him for the asking was more than likely, but if she once let it happen she was lost.

She went upstairs shortly afterwards, ostensibly to sort out the spare bedding, in reality because it was driving her crazy just being in the same room with him. By the time he came up around nine-thirty, she was already in bed, though far from sleep.

The *en suite* bathroom was reached via the dressing room, a fact which hadn't occurred to her earlier. This time she refused to turn away, or even close her eyes while he shed his clothing, just managing not to look at him directly.

Only when he reached the bathroom door did she allow herself a peep, stomach doing a painful flip on sight of the tapering back, the hard male buttocks and thighs. There was no flab anywhere on that body of his, just firm muscle covered by smooth, lightly tanned skin. No normal, red-blooded woman could fail to be stirred by him.

He was still naked when he emerged from the bathroom, although it was only something she sensed, as she didn't dare look at him again. Tense already, she tautened still further as he approached the bed, squeezing her eyes shut in a futile attempt to appear asleep.

'Stop pretending,' he said softly. 'I can feel the heat from here!'

'Get lost!' she muttered through clenched teeth, and heard his low laugh.

'You don't really mean that.'

She kicked out at him as he peeled back the sheet to slide in beside her. Not that there was room for much manoeuvring in a three-foot divan. The grey eyes held a devilish gleam, his mouth an uncompromising purpose. He hauled her to him, holding her against the hard length of his body until she stopped struggling and lay quiescent in his arms, her breath mingling with his as he put his lips to hers, her mind relinquishing the unequal battle.

The hands she had used to try and push him away now stole about his neck, fingers running into the thick dark hair, relishing the crisp clean feel of it. Time had ceased to exist; she was back in the past, her instincts taking over, tongue meeting his, tasting, twining, drawing away in tantalising invitation, hips moving slowly and gently, feeling the mounting pressure, hearing his breathing roughen.

Wrapped tightly about her in the struggle, her nightdress was a barrier she wanted urgently to disappear, yet Kyle was making no attempt to take it from her. He seemed almost to be holding back.

'All or nothing,' he murmured against her lips.

What he wanted was her total surrender, came the thought as sense and sensibility returned in a rush. A sop to his male ego, nothing more!

'Nothing, then!' she gritted, fighting the part of her that inclined towards paying the price regardless. 'I'm not *that* desperate!'

For a lengthy moment he was still, hands warm at her back, body registering an unmistakable arousal. She was stunned when he let go of her and slid from the bed again, unable to believe that he wasn't going to carry on when he was so obviously stimulated—her own ego flattened by the realisation that he didn't find her irresistible even at this stage.

Unselfconscious in his virile male nudity, he studied her with cynicism. 'You will be,' he promised. 'I'm going to make sure of it.'

She came up on an elbow as he moved away, smothering the urge to call him back. 'Don't count on it!' she called after him.

He didn't bother to answer. Shannon collapsed back into the pillows as the communicating door closed between them, feeling the unrelieved ache in her body and cursing her own weakness in allowing him to get to her at all. One thing was certain. She would *not* be giving him the satisfaction of hearing her beg him to make love to her. She'd as soon cut her tongue out first!

She slept through sheer exhaustion in the end, waking to the dazzling brightness of sunshine on snow, and the distant sound of laughter.

It took a moment or two for the message relayed by

the clock on her bedside table to sink in. Eleven o'clock! It couldn't be!

A glance at the watch she had left in the drawer was confirmation enough. So what? she asked herself, resisting the impulse to jump from the bed and start flinging on clothes. She must have needed the sleep.

Kyle obviously hadn't; she could hear his voice raised in some shouted instruction, followed by another burst of laughter from Jodie. They were outside, she realised.

This time she did get up, padding across to the window to look out on the near lawns, where the two of them were having a snowball fight. Wearing jeans and a cream Aran sweater, hair sparkling wetly in the sunlight, Kyle was pulling no punches against his diminutive opponent, deadly in his aim. Caught fair and square as she peeked from behind a shrub, Jodie promptly scooped up a handful and let fly in return, yelling triumphantly when he failed to sidestep in time.

Hands up in surrender, laughing himself, he shook his head as his niece made to repeat the action. 'Enough,' Shannon understood him to say.

Jodie caught sight of her at the window, and lifted her hand in an enthusiastic wave, small face glowing with health and vitality. Following her gaze, Kyle waved too, the smile curving his lips hinting of mockery.

Shannon turned away, last night's emotional turmoil welling up again inside her. It was no use telling herself she hated him when she knew full well that it wasn't true. He might be all sorts of a louse for doing what he'd done last night, but it made little difference. She could even admire the strength of mind over matter that had enabled him to leave himself unfulfilled in the interests of showing her just who was in charge.

What she couldn't and wouldn't do was let him know how she really felt about him—how she had never stopped feeling about him, if she was honest about it. That would be like putting her head on the block, because he certainly didn't have the same depth of feeling for her. From now on she had to steer clear of any physical contact, however difficult that might prove. It was the only way she was going to get through this affair.

The two of them were back indoors by the time she went down, both looking as if they'd thoroughly enjoyed the morning's entertainment.

'You must come and see our snowman!' said Jodie. 'We built a huge one out near the pond, with buttons for his eyes and a carrot for his nose! Uncle Kyle found a scarf and cap for him to wear too. All he needs now is a mouth, but we couldn't find anything suitable.'

'You could try a banana,' Shannon suggested lightly. 'Or how about cutting one out of cardboard and painting it?'

'The artistic touch,' commented Kyle drily. 'Unfortunately, cardboard tends to turn soggy when wet.'

'Which it's hardly going to get while the frost lasts,' she countered, hanging onto the light note. 'If you can come up with something better, feel free!'

Otherwise, belt up! Unspoken, the words hung in the air between them, accompanied by a challenging green gaze and stubbornly tilted chin. A hint of a smile flickered across his lips as he regarded her.

'Just no putting you down, is there?'

'You can take a bet on it!' she said.

Jodie was watching the pair of them with bright-eyed interest.

Wearing yellow cord jeans and purple shirt, short dark hair brushed into shining order, she looked so different from the waif they had met at the home, Shannon reflected, abandoning her stand. Only on the surface, though. She was still the same dauntless little character underneath.

It would be dangerously easy to get too close. The relationship would be severed in three months' time. It was going to be necessary when the time came to come up with some reasonable explanation as to why she and Kyle were parting, but Jodie would no doubt accept it as she accepted everything—with resilience. Kyle would be the one stable factor in her life.

They had omelettes for lunch. Made by Kyle, naturally. Like everything he tackled, they were perfect: light and fluffy and delicious. Shannon refused to feel any shame over her own lack of talent in that direction. He liked to cook, she didn't; why go against nature?

She made up for it by clearing the table and loading the dishwasher afterwards, then spent a few minutes drawing the mouth shape on a piece of stiffish cardboard torn from a cereal packet, for Jodie to cut out. They couldn't find any suitably coloured paint, so made do with a blue marker pen to draw in some teeth, and a red one for the tongue Jodie insisted on finishing off with.

'Should give any would-be burglars a fright, if nothing else,' Kyle observed, when shown the masterpiece. 'Those map markers are made to glow in the dark.'

'Great!' said his niece, even more enthused. 'I'll be able to see it from my bedroom window!'

'I'll come with you to help fix it on,' offered Shannon, reluctant to be alone with Kyle. 'Just give me a minute to get my things.'

She had forgotten about her restricted wardrobe. Apart from an ancient anorak left over from her teens, and an equally old pair of brogues, there was nothing here suitable for deep-snow wear. She would just have to steer clear of the deeper bits, she reasoned, not about to be put off by minor detail.

She exchanged the black and white checked skirt she was wearing for a pair of ski trousers that were the same tone of red as her sweater, and tucked her hair up under a woolly pull-on hat before donning the off-white anorak. The image she presented was hardly out of the fashion pages, but who cared? She wasn't out to impress anyone.

Jodie had waited for her, though only just. Shannon didn't blame her for being impatient. Her own childhood wasn't so long ago that she couldn't remember feeling the same way about the time it took adults to get ready for anything.

They left Kyle immersed in the morning newspaper, which he had only just got round to opening, and made their way through the garden to where the snowman stood close by the iced-up pond. Shannon attempted to keep to the trodden-down areas to start with, but gave up after sinking above her ankles when she slipped off the hidden path into an equally hidden flowerbed. If her feet got wet, they got wet; they were hardly going to develop frostbite.

The snowman, she had to admit, was an excellent creation, complete with moulded arms and sturdy legs. With the mouth fixed *in situ*, he looked positively fearsome. Enough to scare the daylights out of anybody coming on him by chance after dark.

'Do you think you're going to be happy here, Jodie?' she asked on a casual note when they eventually started back to the house. 'It's a lot different from Brisbane.'

The small face acquired a sudden shuttered look. 'I don't want to go back there.'

'You won't be going back,' Shannon hastened to assure her. 'This is your home now. Once the adoption goes through, you'll be Jodie Beaumont, not Brent.'

Grey eyes regained their brightness. 'I'm going to be adopted?'

'Of course.' Shannon kept her tone easy.

'So I'll have two parents, like other kids?'

Shannon hardly knew what to say to that. It was obvious she had been taking far too much for granted in assuming that Jodie would just accept the situation when the time came. Self-centredness on her part, she was bound to acknowledge. Not that recognising it helped at all.

'Lots of children only have one parent,' she said cautiously. 'Sometimes, it can even work out just as well.'

'Only if they care,' was the heartbreakingly unemotional answer. 'Dad didn't want me. I cost too much, he always said.' She winged a glance at her, the irrepressible spirit breaking through. 'I've cost Uncle Kyle a fortune already, haven't I?'

'Getting on that way,' Shannon agreed, shelving the problem for now. 'But worth every penny!'

The grin was pure mischief. 'Want to bet?' She sprang into sudden action. 'Race you back!'

They arrived at the house neck to neck, falling into the rear lobby laughing and pushing one another like a couple of kids.

Shannon peeled off her wet shoes, along with the wetter socks, padding through to the kitchen in bare feet to loose her hair from the confines of the woolly hat, her face, like Jodie's own, aglow.

'It's been years since I did that,' she claimed, pleased to have proved herself up to scratch on the energy front. 'I bet I can beat you next time!'

Jodie gave her an indulgent look. 'No chance! I wasn't even trying.'

'Little horror!' Shannon pretended to go for her, promptly skidded on a patch of mush tramped in on

Jodie's wellingtons, and finished up on her back halfway
under the table with her legs tangled up in a chair.

'Rather more duck than swan,' commented Kyle from
the doorway.

'Ducks are more fun than swans,' declared a highly
diverted Jodie.

'Tell me about it.' He came to shift the chair and haul
Shannon none too gently to her feet, his expression lacking genuine amusement. 'Anything damaged?'

The time to ask that should have been before handling
her like a sack of coals, not after, she felt like telling
him caustically, but, with Jodie looking on, plumped for
a wry laugh instead. 'Only my dignity!'

'You'd better compose yourself, then,' he said. 'We
have a visitor.'

It was the tone more than the words themselves that
registered. She gazed at him in slowly growing dismay
as suspicion crystallised into certainty. Craig was here!

CHAPTER SEVEN

IT HARDLY mattered, but she asked anyway, playing for time to adjust. 'When?'

'A few minutes ago. Said he was in the area, so thought he'd take the opportunity to make a call.' Kyle ran a sardonic eye over her finger-raked blonde hair, flushed cheeks and mouth minus any trace of lipstick. 'You might want to tidy yourself up first.'

Shannon lifted her chin, giving him back look for look. 'I feel fine as I am, thanks.' She lightened her tone deliberately. 'Come and meet a friend, Jodie.'

Craig was in the front sitting room, perfectly at ease. He took in the details of her appearance with obvious surprise. The first time he'd seen her looking anything but well-groomed, of course.

He looked as he always did—handsome, stylishly clad, teak-brown hair kept in trim by the best. Both shorter and lighter in build than Kyle, he showed no sign of being overpowered by the other man's presence.

'I thought I'd pop in to see you while I was so close,' he said.

'Nice of you to take the time,' Shannon returned with a composure that was all surface. 'This is Jodie. Mr Ramsey, Jodie.'

Grey eyes gave the newcomer a swift scrutiny, conclusions, if any, kept under wraps. 'Hi,' she said.

Craig turned on the charm he was famed for, his smile indulgent. 'Hi to you too! How are you?'

There was no answering smile, just a steady gaze and

a self-contained 'Okay'. She looked back at Shannon. 'Can I go and watch television in the other room?'

'If you want to.' A stupid answer, Shannon acknowledged ruefully, considering the request made. 'How about a drink?' she suggested as the girl left the room.

Craig shook his head. 'Not for me, thanks. I'm driving.'

'I meant coffee or tea. I was planning on making some anyway.' An outright lie, but who was to know it?

'Oh, in that case, yes,' he agreed. 'Coffee for me, please. Decaff, if you have it.'

'I'll have full strength,' said Kyle.

Just to be awkward, Shannon thought fumingly, wishing she'd kept her mouth shut. There were times when the social courtesies were best left ignored.

She took a moment to find a pair of pumps in the hall cupboard before getting to work, wondering what on earth Craig hoped to achieve by turning up out of the blue like this. She had surely made the situation clear enough already.

Wheeling the trolley through some minutes later, she found Kyle in the same stance by the fireplace, hands thrust into trouser pockets, expression inscrutable. Craig was sitting, though looking a little less at ease. Shannon handed out the cups, offered the plate of biscuits, which nobody wanted, and took a seat herself, eyeing the two men in growing exasperation when neither made any attempt to speak.

'I thought I'd explained everything on the phone yesterday, Craig,' she said at length.

'You did.' He paused, lifting his shoulders in a faintly defensive shrug. 'I wanted to see you.'

'What you really mean,' put in Kyle shortly, 'is you wanted to see what was going on. In other words, you don't have a lot of faith in her.'

The other man shook his head, mouth compressed. 'That's not true. I have every faith. What I can't accept is the way you're making her party to a serious deception. I've every sympathy for the child through there, but it's *your* problem, not Shannon's. You had no right to involve her.'

Grey eyes narrowed dangerously. 'Is that a fact?'

'Stop it, both of you!' Shannon was too angry for diplomacy, sitting forward on the edge of her seat, the red of her sweater echoed in the spots of colour burning high on her cheekbones. 'I'm not a chattel! I make my own decisions! If you're finding it difficult to accept the situation, Craig, then I'm sorry, but it's something I have to go through with.'

The pause was both lengthy and heavy. Kyle's face was impassive, Craig's taking on resignation.

'I still think you're wrong, but it seems I don't have a choice,' he said. 'Just so long as I'm not expected to spend the next three months without any contact at all.'

Shannon allowed herself no time for reflection. 'Of course not. We already arranged to meet on Wednesday, didn't we?'

Glancing Kyle's way, Craig seemed about to say something else, then apparently thought better of it, fastening his attention on the mantel clock. 'I'd better be going. I'm supposed to be in Redhill by five.'

Shannon got to her feet, careful not to look in Kyle's direction. 'I'll see you off.'

She waited until they were in the hall before giving vent to her feelings.

'You shouldn't have come, Craig. It doesn't help anything!'

'I had to,' he said flatly. 'I needed to see for myself how things really were.'

Shannon wished she only knew herself. 'And what conclusions have you reached?' she asked, eyes veiled.

'I think that husband of yours is going to do everything he can to split us up.'

Her heart missed a beat, then steadied again. 'Why would he do that?'

'Because he needs you to look after the child. Not that I imagine he'd be averse to a renewal of marital relations too, of course.'

'He'd have to tie me down first!' she claimed, wishing she could be as certain as she sounded. 'There's no chance of my staying on once the adoption is settled. I've my own life to lead.'

Craig gave her an approving nod. 'Keep thinking that way.'

He kissed her lingeringly at the door. Closing it on him, Shannon stood for a moment or two to steady her thoughts. Craig was right, of course. Kyle needed a long-term mother for Jodie if she was to have the life he wanted for her, and who better than a wife who not only had a regard for the child already, but was still physically desirable? He wouldn't even need to repeat his marriage vows—for what difference they'd made to start with.

If it wasn't for Jodie, she wouldn't hesitate—but then, if it wasn't for Jodie, she wouldn't be here at all. She was going around in circles, she concluded wryly. What it came down to was, did she put the child's interests before her own?

She went back to the sitting room with that question unanswered. Kyle had drawn the drapes across and switched on a couple of lamps. He regarded her with irony.

'Definitely not your type,' he stated.

'Obviously not yours,' she countered. 'And I'm not going to start discussing rival merits.'

The irony deepened. 'You do credit *me* with some, then?'

'Of course.' Shannon moved to start gathering cups and saucers, glad of the excuse. 'There aren't that many men who'd go to the trouble you're going to.'

'I'll do whatever it takes,' he said. 'So will you in the end.'

One of the cups fell over with a rattle as she placed it on the trolley, spilling the dregs of coffee left in the bottom. She righted it carefully, mopping up the spillage with a napkin while she sought an adequate response.

'You take too much for granted,' was all she could come up with.

'I don't think so. You don't have it in you to walk out on a relationship you're already well into establishing.'

Shannon pushed her hair back out of her eyes with an unsteady hand. 'I can always visit.'

'No substitute. Not one I'm prepared to accept anyway.'

'You'll have to.' She started pushing the trolley towards the door, coming to a halt as he moved to intercept. This time she did look at him, eyes fired. 'I mean it, Kyle!'

'So do I,' he said with deadly softness. 'I won't let you go to him, Shannon. You're needed here.'

Standing there, tall, dark and immovable, he made her pulses race. 'What about *my* needs?' she demanded thickly, and saw his mouth slant.

'I'll take care of those.'

'You think sex is all there is to it!' she jerked out. 'Well, I can tell you, it comes pretty far down *my* list of priorities!'

'I'd have said it was pretty near the top last night.'

The mockery galvanised her into retaliation with the only weapon immediately to hand. Kyle caught the viciously shoved trolley before it reached its target, ignoring the teetering, rattling contents as he turned it aside with a flick of a strong brown wrist, an unholy gleam in his eyes.

'Action stations, is it?'

Shannon made a futile attempt to evade the arm he shot out to grab her, pummelling at his chest with both fists as he pulled her to him. Like trying to hold off a bulldozer, came the fleeting thought, for all the impression made. He lifted her clear of the floor, the mouth seeking hers deadly in its aim, smothering her protests.

She was helpless in his grasp—equally helpless to stop the swift-rising tide of emotion. His kisses had always stirred her beyond the realms of reason, cutting out everything but the feel of his lips, his body, his sheer vitality.

Somehow she found herself lying in his arms on the sofa, his hand at her breast beneath the red sweater, lean features dark and passionate in the lamplight.

'*Now* try telling me this isn't important to you!' he said. 'Try telling me you don't get anything at all out of my touching you. That this—' he smoothed the ball of his thumb over her tingling, aching nipple '—is how you always are!'

'I didn't say it wasn't important to me,' Shannon murmured huskily. 'I said there were other things even more important.'

'I agree,' he said. 'Jodie's welfare, for one. I'll move heaven and earth if necessary to give her what she's missed all these years.'

'You can do that anyway.'

'No, I can't. Not enough. She's going to need a

woman to turn to—someone who's been through all the physical and emotional transitions she's going to be experiencing before too long.' The grey eyes were intent on her face, assessing the effect both words and action were having on her. 'Think about how it would have been for you without a mother to talk to.'

Shannon caught at the marauding hand, unable to think at all while he was doing that. 'You're asking me to give up everything I've got together for myself this last eighteen months,' she said desperately. 'Including Craig.'

His lips thinned. 'Would that be so much of a sacrifice?'

'Of course it would!'

'You're telling me you're in love with him?' He shook his head when she hesitated. 'As I said, not so much of a sacrifice. You'd have been bored out of your mind within a month if you'd married him.'

He ran his free hand through the thickness of her hair, cupping the back of her head to hold her still, forcing her to look at him directly. 'There's a chance it will all fall through if you leave. Could you live with yourself if it did, knowing you could have stopped it?'

'*You* stop it!' Her voice was ragged. 'I won't let you do this to me, Kyle!'

'I'm just pointing out what you already know,' he said. 'What you've known since you agreed to take the whole thing on. You didn't do it *just* for Jodie's sake.'

'Meaning I saw it as a way of getting back with you?'

'It's not beyond the realms of possibility.'

She gave a brittle little laugh. 'If there's one thing that doesn't alter, it's the size of your ego!'

'But you're not denying it,' he said levelly. 'No more than I'd deny wanting you back.'

'Want I might go for. Just don't try making out it's anything beyond that—for either of us!'

He made no attempt, a certain ruefulness in his faint smile. 'We could still make it work.'

'We didn't last time.'

'We didn't try hard enough. Either of us,' he added before she could voice the protest.

'It wasn't me who went off the rails!' Shannon pointed out.

'It wasn't...' Kyle caught himself up, jaw setting. 'I'm not going over all that again. What matters is here and now.'

If they hadn't run into Paula yesterday—if she hadn't been forcibly reminded of his capacity for deception—she might have given in. As it was, she had to bring every ounce of will-power she possessed to bear in order to form a rejection.

'It's no use, Kyle. Much as I feel for Jodie, I'm not big enough to sacrifice everything *I* want from life for her. You'll just have to find someone else to see her through puberty.'

There was no lessening of purpose in the grey eyes. 'You'll change your mind,' he said.

Shannon knew an involuntary dissension as he withdrew his hand from her to get up, and knew he was aware of it too. He held the most potent weapons in this battle of theirs. How long could she hope to hold firm against them when she was so weak to start with?

They went to a local restaurant they had used in the past for dinner, to be greeted by the proprietor as long-lost friends.

'I thought you must have moved house,' he remarked, taking it on himself to bring the wine Kyle ordered. 'It must be a couple of years since you were here last.'

'About that,' Kyle agreed easily, obviously seeing no reason to expound on the whys and wherefores. 'How's business these days?'

The man pulled a face. 'Not too bad, though the double yellows don't help any.'

'What's double yellows?' asked Jodie, mystified.

'They're lines painted at the roadside to stop cars parking there,' he told her.

'If they're only painted, why can't the cars just park on top of them?' was the practical response, drawing a wry laugh.

'Why indeed!' A couple who to his knowledge had been childless a couple of years ago turning up with a nine-year-old Aussie in tow had to arouse some curiosity on his part, but he made no comment, contenting himself with a pleasant, 'Enjoy your meal.'

'So why can't they?' Jodie insisted as he moved away, not prepared to accept 'Why indeed!' as any kind of answer.

'Because it's against regulations,' said Shannon.

'The road outside here is too narrow for traffic to pass safely when cars are parked,' Kyle clarified.

An explanation she would have done better to give herself rather than the bald statement of fact, Shannon acknowledged ruefully. Kyle credited the child with the intelligence to comprehend. Which she had, of course.

He would be good both to and for her; about that there was no doubt. She was already developing a real regard for him; it was there in her eyes when she looked at him—although caution still crept in at times too. It was all too good to last, Shannon could imagine her thinking. Only when the adoption formalities were completed might she start to trust in the permanency of this new life.

A trust she herself was planning to destroy, came the sombre reminder.

It was gone nine when they got back to the house. Jodie stuck her chin out when it was suggested that she go to bed soon after, but she obviously wasn't sure enough of her position as yet to start putting up any real objections. Shannon could hardly blame her for feeling a little rebellious. Her father probably hadn't cared what time she went to bed, just providing she didn't get in his way.

'Considering it's Monday tomorrow, I'd have thought she might be wondering about school,' she said to Kyle.

'Maybe hoping that if she doesn't mention it no one else will,' he returned on a humorous note. 'I think we'd better prepare her for the inevitable. We're due to see the principal at Silverwood on Wednesday morning.'

Lounging there in the chair, legs comfortably stretched, he looked and sounded totally relaxed. Far more than she was, Shannon reflected wryly, wishing she could be as impervious to his charms as he appeared to be to hers at the moment.

He had taken off his tie and opened the collar of his shirt for ease, revealing the strong brown column of his throat. She had an urgent desire to go and put her lips where the curl of hair began—to rouse him the way he was rousing her, just for the hell of it.

It took a moment or two for the latter statement to penetrate. 'I'm meeting Craig for lunch Wednesday,' she said.

'No, you're not.'

The calm statement aroused very different instincts, tilting her chin and triggering an angry glitter. 'Just how do you propose stopping me?'

A smile flickered across his lips. 'I shan't need to stop you. You've about as much intention of marrying Craig as I have, and it's time you told him so. Unless you'd rather I did it for you?'

'You stay away from him!' Poised now on the very edge of her chair, body taut as a bow-string, Shannon almost spat the words out. 'It's not up to you to tell him anything!'

'It shouldn't be, I agree, but if I have to I will.' The tone was still even, but the determination was evident. 'You're married to me, and you're staying married to me. I'll put every obstacle I can find in the way of a divorce.'

She gazed at him impotently, a hard obstruction in her throat. 'You really would do anything for Jodie, wouldn't you?' she got out.

'Not just for Jodie,' he said. His voice softened, plucking at her heartstrings. 'For all of us.'

It would be easy, too fatally easy, to go along with him, Shannon acknowledged. A man who would go to the lengths he was willing to go to in order to secure a child's future had to be worth loving, regardless of what else he might or might not be.

She tensed afresh as he got purposefully to his feet, recognising his intention. 'Don't,' she said, but there was no force in it.

He didn't waste any more breath on words, simply scooped her up from the chair. Shannon turned her face into the broad chest as he carried her to the door. It still wasn't too late to back out, but she knew she wasn't going to. Not now. Whatever the outcome, she was stuck with it.

They undressed each other, dropping the garments where they stood. Shannon pressed her lips to the hollow of his throat, quivering as the firm, long-fingered hands re-established their claim on her body. Her own hands followed the same route down over hard-ridged muscle and flat male hip to find the source of his masculinity, feeling him shudder to her caress: steel in velvet, pulsing with life and promise.

King-sized, the bed received the two of them with familiarity. She wrapped long legs about him when they came together, cherishing the never-forgotten feel of him inside her, filling her, possessing her.

'Again!' she whispered before the world had fully steadied, and heard his low laugh.

'Insatiable as ever!'

Only for you, she wanted to tell him, but the words stuck in her throat. 'Do you need more time?' she said instead, and he laughed again, rolling to bring her on top of him, lean features taunting.

'Does this feel like it? And *this*!'

The laughter faded as he viewed the slender, lamp-bronzed stretch of her body, his hands moving up from her hips to cup the firm jut of her breasts, the flame in his eyes a reflection of the fire still burning inside her. She arched her back to bring the curves into greater prominence, sliding her hands beneath the heavy mane of blonde hair at her nape with slow sensuality—seeing the flame become an all-consuming blaze.

Kyle must have switched off the lamp before going to sleep himself, because it was dark when Shannon opened her eyes again, although a glimmer of light showed through the chink where the curtains hadn't quite met.

He was still there at her side, an arm thrown over her waist, one leg curved across hers, his breathing deep and easy. She studied the strong, clean lines of his face, remembering the feel of his lips on her body, the expression in his eyes. In that way nothing had changed; she had always been able to stir him physically. What she hadn't before and still couldn't plumb was the inner man. Maybe she never would.

Mistake or not, there was no going back on the decision now, although it wasn't going to be easy telling Craig. Kyle was right, of course; she had known from the moment they met up again that the marriage was out of the question. She should have had the guts to come clean yesterday. The hurt might have been no less, but at least he wouldn't be under any illusions still.

It had to be face to face, anyway. Kyle would have to go along with that. If Wednesday was out, then she had to set up another meeting—the sooner the better.

The clock was on Kyle's side of the bed, and impossible to see clearly from this distance. Heaven only knew what time it was! She made a tentative attempt to slide from beneath the encircling arm without disturbing him, subsiding again as the grey eyes opened.

Recollection was instantaneous, his smile heart-stirring.

'Sleep well?' he asked softly.

'I must have,' she said, trying to sound as easy as he did about it. 'It's light outside. If Jodie's already up, she'll be wondering what happened to us.'

'Considering her background, she'll probably have a very good idea, unfortunately,' Kyle observed, running the tip of a finger slowly across her lips. There was a moment when he looked on the verge of going further, then he pressed a swift kiss on the end of her nose and rolled away to sit up, giving vent to an exclamation as he saw the time. 'It's a quarter to nine!'

Shannon resisted the urge to reach out and run her fingers down the bare back presented to her as he flung back the covers and swung his feet to the floor. 'Looks like the jet-lag finally caught up on us,' she said. 'Maybe it did on Jodie too.'

'Maybe.' He turned to look at her, eyes kindling again as they moved from the tumbled blonde hair and provocative face down over smooth bare shoulders to the swell of her breasts. 'Better not count on it, though. She might come looking for us. Why don't you go and check on her while I'm in the shower?'

He made for the dressing room, not bothering to don the robe lying across the foot of the bed. Watching him, Shannon felt a sudden stab beneath her ribs at the thought that Paula would have seen him like this too. And how many others?

She would never be able to trust him, she acknowledged ruefully. In giving way to him, she was risking being hurt again—but what choice had he given her?

The sharp knock on the outer door made her jump. She pulled the bedclothes hastily up over her bare breasts before issuing an invitation, summoning a smile for the girl who appeared round the door bearing a tray.

'What's this, then?'

'Breakfast,' Jodie answered, sounding as if it should be self-evident. 'I've been up ages!'

'Oh, sweetheart, I'm sorry!' Shannon felt a complete heel. 'You should have woken us!'

'That's okay,' came the unperturbed response. 'I had some cereal, and made a bacon sandwich. I've done some more for you and Uncle Kyle.

'Where is he?' she added, setting down the tray.

'In the shower.' Shannon gazed in fascination at the doorstep sandwiches residing on the two plates, wondering how she was going to manage to even get her mouth round one. 'It's really thoughtful of you, Jodie.'

'They're dead easy to do,' she said, obviously taking it that even grilling bacon was a little beyond her. 'Specially if you get some sliced bread in. I'll take Uncle Kyle's to him, shall I?'

'You could go and knock on the bathroom door to tell him,' Shannon advised hastily as the other plate was lifted.

Jodie gave her what could only be termed an old-fashioned look. 'I've seen Dad without any clothes on plenty of times.'

Shannon didn't doubt it. That father of hers had possessed few if any sensibilities.

'It's different with uncles,' was all she could come up with. 'In fact, I'd better tell him myself.'

She made to get out of bed, stopping abruptly at the realisation that she wasn't wearing anything either. Jodie regarded her solemnly.

'Is it different with aunts too?'

It was ridiculous to be self-conscious in front of the girl, Shannon told herself firmly. Nudity was natural after all. 'Not really,' she said, and got to her feet. 'I shan't be a minute.'

She could feel the younger but no less appraising grey eyes on her back as she moved to the dressing room door, and was relieved despite herself to gain a little privacy. Jodie was altogether too worldly for a nine-year-old. At some point, either she or Kyle would need to have a serious talk with her about how much of that worldliness should be revealed when it came to mixing with others her own age.

Her wrap was on the divan where she had left it. She put it on before going to the bathroom door. Kyle would laugh at her if she knocked instead of just going in, she knew, but she still felt some hesitation about doing it after all this time.

He was shaving at the long mirror over the double basins, a towel wrapped low about his hips.

'Nearly finished,' he said. 'Jodie still asleep?'

Shannon shook her head, unable to tear her eyes away

from the sleekly muscled, superbly fit body. There were faint red marks on his back where her nails had dug in last night. Meeting the grey eyes in the mirror, she felt her stomach turn over, her pulses start throbbing again.

'She brought us breakfast in bed,' she said, unsurprised to hear the huskiness in her voice. 'Bacon sandwiches.'

He laughed. 'Hot ones, I hope.'

'They must have been to start with. I doubt if they are still.'

Kyle wiped away the last of the shaving foam, and reached for the silk robe thrown over the nearby chair. 'I suppose we'd better go and get them, then, before they totally congeal.'

'Wait a minute.' Her fingers were unsteady as they touched the firm warm flesh. 'I seem to have got a bit rough last night.'

He said softly, 'Who's complaining?'

Unable to stop herself, she put her lips to the spot, sliding her hands about his waist to trace the hard ridging of stomach muscle, her nostrils filled with the clean fresh masculine scent of him.

He said something low in his throat, and turned to pull her to him, kissing her all too briefly before putting her firmly away from him again, lips slanting.

'Enticing, but needs must. Tell Jodie I'll be right out.'

She hadn't set out to entice him, Shannon wanted to say, but she wasn't sure it was true. In those few tumultuous minutes she had forgotten all about Jodie out there waiting for them, concerned only with her own overriding desires.

She felt even worse on finding Jodie gone from the bedroom, having left the sandwiches sitting accusingly on the tray. Following her through, now clad in the silk robe, Kyle eyed them with the same lack of enthusiasm.

'I suppose we ought to make some effort.'

'I don't think I can,' Shannon admitted. 'Not cold bacon. Couldn't we just pretend to have eaten them?'

'Hardly fair after she went to the trouble.' Kyle lifted one of the hefty slabs and took a bite, chewing on it manfully. 'We won't be able to have anything else for breakfast if we're not to hurt her feelings any more than we already did.'

'Some sacrifices I'm prepared to make,' Shannon said firmly. 'I'll wrap mine in tissues for now, and get rid of it later. It doesn't detract from the thought.'

She took the plate with her through to the bathroom, leaving him still making gallant inroads into his own sandwich. The only place to put the wrapped parcel was in the waste bin, although she must remember to remove it before Mrs Parkin came to clean upstairs.

The latter always used to arrive around nine-thirty, which had to be any minute now. Kyle would have prepared her for the new state of affairs, of course, but there was certain to be some initial awkwardness. Just one more hurdle to cross.

He had already left when she returned to the bedroom after her shower, the empty plate left on the tray. He'd do anything rather than hurt the child, Shannon reflected, unable to stifle a pang. Last night had been wonderful, only there was a difference between merely making love and loving. Jodie was the one who really mattered to him.

Better to have him in part than not have him at all, she concluded, forcing herself to look on the up side. She'd spent the last eighteen months missing him like crazy, even if she hadn't been prepared to admit it at the time. Anything had to be better than continuing that way.

Almost anything, at any rate.

CHAPTER EIGHT

SHANNON used the telephone in the bedroom to phone her parents, unsurprised by the aggrieved note in her mother's voice when she realised who was calling.

'We've been waiting to hear from you all weekend! You might at least have let us know you were safely back in the country!'

'I'm sorry, Mom,' Shannon said penitently. 'It was thoughtless of me.'

'Well, I suppose you've had other things to think about.' There was a pause, a change of tone. 'How is everything, anyway?'

Shannon lightened her own tone. 'Fine! Jodie's been having a wonderful time in the snow. The first time she ever saw the stuff outside of the cinema. She's a real character! Dad will be tickled pink with her.'

'We're looking forward to meeting her.' Lucy Holroyd paused again. 'What about you and Kyle?'

Asked that same question yesterday, Shannon would have been forced to prevaricate. Even now, she found herself hesitating a moment before taking the plunge.

'We decided to start over.'

'Oh, that's wonderful! I can't tell you how happy it makes me! I know Kyle did a bad thing, but anyone can make a mistake. That woman was mostly to blame anyway! Women who make up to married men should be ashamed of themselves!'

'It takes two,' Shannon commented drily.

'Oh, I know, darling, but men are so much more easily led astray. When can we expect to see you? Your father's taking a week's break right now, so any day will suit us. All three of you, of course.'

'I'll discuss it with Kyle and let you know,' Shannon promised, unwilling to commit herself. 'Talk to you later.'

She replaced the receiver, sitting there for a moment in silent contemplation. Her things still had to be transferred from the spare room, but there was more to think about than just that. If she and Kyle were back together for the foreseeable future, there was the flat to be considered.

Giving the place up would be a wrench, but keeping it on was purposeless if she really intended staying the course. Which she did. She had to. For herself now as much as for Jodie.

Wearing a pair of silky trousers and a loose top, she went downstairs to the sound of vacuuming coming from the direction of the sitting room. She had always got on well with Mrs Parkin in the past, but still felt awkward about seeing her again after all this time. Judging by the spotless state of the house, the woman had been coming in on a regular basis, which seemed to indicate that Kyle had spent a fair amount of time here.

If he and Paula hadn't actually cohabited, that wasn't to say they'd never spent a night here together, of course. The sudden thought that they might even have shared the same bed she and Kyle had shared last night was like probing an open wound.

Shannon took a grip on herself. What was past was past. With Jodie to consider, Kyle would surely think twice before rocking the boat again.

She found the two of them appropriately enough in the morning room. Kyle was standing at the window, hands thrust into trouser pockets as he gazed out on the wintry scene. He turned when she came into the room, a smile curving his lips.

'I was beginning to think you'd gone back to bed.'

'I had some things to sort out,' Shannon answered lightly, dismayed to feel herself actually blushing at the reminiscent look in the grey eyes. She was married to the man, for heaven's sake! They'd done nothing they hadn't done many times before.

Nothing he hadn't done with other women, for sure, came the thought, hastily thrust aside.

Sprawled on the floor with one of the books they had bought her on Saturday, Jodie hadn't looked up. The way she was flicking over the pages, reading wasn't exactly one of her favourite pastimes, Shannon gathered. How well she could read at all was a matter to be assessed along with the rest. It wouldn't be her fault if she turned out to be below par for her age.

'Sorry we were such a long time coming to get the sandwiches,' she said, crossing her fingers behind her back for the white lie coming. 'They were very good.'

'S'all right,' was the stoical response. 'I suppose you were having sex.'

Totally thrown, Shannon could find no reply to that. It seemed probable that allowing his young daughter to see him nude was the least of Trevor Brent's trespasses. She stole a glance at Kyle, to find him sharing similar thoughts if his expression was anything to go by.

'What do you know about sex?' he asked without force.

'We had lessons about it at school. It's what men and women do to make babies.' The tone was matter-of-fact. 'Only when they want to, though. That's why Dad didn't make any more after me.' Jodie looked up, gaze going from uncle to aunt contemplatively. 'Haven't you ever wanted to make one?'

Shannon felt her heart jerk. 'We've been too busy,' she said. 'Anyway, we've got you now.'

'*I'm* not a baby,' Jodie pointed out. 'I wouldn't mind if you did make one,' she added after a moment. 'I like babies.'

For Shannon, the bleeping of the telephone was a relief. 'Worth considering,' said Kyle softly as she moved to answer it.

She would have to be a great deal surer of him than she was as yet before *she* considered it, she thought, lifting the receiver. More than half expecting the call to be her mother ringing back with something she had forgotten to say, as so often happened, she didn't bother giving the number, offering a simple 'Hello'.

Only it wasn't her mother. There was a brief silence after she spoke, then a decisive click as of a receiver being replaced.

Kyle eyed her questioningly as she slowly replaced her own receiver. 'Wrong number?'

'So it seems,' she said. 'Whoever it was didn't speak.'

She could have imagined the fleeting change of expression in the grey eyes, but she had a strong suspicion that he knew who had been on the other end of that line. Someone who had been expecting him to answer, not her.

'I'll go and make some coffee while I'm up,' she announced, needing a reason to get out of the room, away from that all-too-penetrative gaze. 'Hot chocolate for you, Jodie?'

Mrs Parkin hadn't yet reached the kitchen. Shannon made the coffee and chocolate on automatic pilot, trying to maintain a rational outlook. It could have been a genuine wrong number; not everyone had the courtesy to acknowledge the fact. On the other hand, people like that usually thudded the receiver down right away. There had been an element of surprise—even shock—in the silence.

Whatever the reason for Paula's exit, Kyle almost certainly hadn't gone without female company since. If that had been some woman on the line, then it obviously wasn't one expecting to hear another woman's voice.

There was a way of at least discovering the caller's number, of course—providing she did it now, before anyone else called. Unable to resist the temptation, Shannon lifted the kitchen receiver and dialled the four digits, copying down the recorded detail on the notepad rather than accept the invitation to press button three and have the call reconnected immediately.

Prefixed by the inner London code, the number meant nothing to her. If she rang it, she might at least learn whether the caller had been male or female. She was standing there irresolute when Mrs Parkin came into the kitchen.

In her late fifties, and looking very little different in the smart blue overall from the last time Shannon had seen her, the woman shook her head in smiling reproof.

'I'd have made that for you if you'd given me a call,' she said. 'Nice to have you back again, anyway.'

Shannon returned the smile, grateful for the unconstrained acceptance. 'Thanks. It's good to find you still with us.'

'Mr Beaumont wanted me to keep coming in even when he wasn't here,' the other confided. 'Not that there's ever a lot needs doing when he is here. A very tidy man, is Mr Beaumont!'

'I imagine just keeping the dust down is a full-time job,' Shannon commented. 'I'd hate to think I'd got it to do myself.'

The older woman laughed. 'Each to their own. I wouldn't know where to start writing a book! Mr

Beaumont was right in the middle of one when he heard about young Jodie through there. She seems to be settling down well already. Amazing how quickly children accept things, isn't it? You'd think—'

She broke off as the doorbell rang, added succinctly, 'Are you in or out?'

'In,' Shannon answered after a momentary pause.

She moved to the kitchen door as Mrs Parkin went to answer the summons, viewing the young woman admitted with a sudden tension.

'Maxine Gregson,' announced the latter briskly. 'Sorry to drop in on you without warning. I was passing the area so I thought I'd take the opportunity. You did know someone would be calling round, of course?'

This had to be the social worker Kyle had spoken of, Shannon realised in something approaching relief. They certainly didn't waste any time! Had she given it any thought at all, she would have expected someone a good deal older. The newcomer was no more than mid-twenties, her casual clothing and long brown hair in no way suggesting officialdom.

'We were just about to have coffee,' she said. 'Would you like some?'

'Love it!' confirmed the other. 'It's bitterly cold this morning. Not that you'd know it in here, of course.'

'I'll set another cup and bring the tray,' offered Mrs Parkin. 'You go on through.'

Seated now, and apparently deep in conversation with the child still sprawled on the floor, Kyle broke off what he was saying when the two of them entered the room, coming to his feet to regard the newcomer with speculation.

Shannon had seen the look that sprang in Maxine's eyes too many times in the past not to recognise it. In the silver-grey trousers and pale blue sweater, features carved by a master craftsman, he was enough to make any female heart beat faster.

'Miss Gregson,' she introduced. 'Here to interview us about the adoption.'

'Maxine, please,' said the girl. 'Max, for short. It's Shannon and Kyle, isn't it? We usually find it better to be on informal terms from the start.'

'I'm sure you're right,' Kyle said easily. 'Let me take your coat.'

She shook her head. 'I'm only going to be here a few minutes this time. I'll just sling it over the back of a chair for now.'

Mrs Parkin came in with the tray as she was doing so. Without being asked, Jodie got up to come and get her chocolate, taking a seat at Shannon's side on the sofa, pixie face set. Shannon poured the coffee and handed it out, giving the still silent Jodie a reassuring smile as she regained her seat.

'We weren't expecting this quite so soon,' Kyle remarked. 'We only got back Saturday.'

'We like to make contact as soon as possible,' the girl answered. 'I realise it's an intrusion, but I'm afraid it's procedure. I'll be calling in several times during the next few weeks, just to see how everything is going with you all.' She gave Jodie a smile, unfazed by the lack of return. 'We have to make sure you're well looked after.

'Not that I anticipate any problems along those lines here,' she added, sweeping a glance over Shannon to linger on Kyle again. 'I understand you went all the way to Australia to save your niece from being put in a home out there.'

'I *was* in a home,' Jodie chimed in. 'I didn't like it.'

'Well, you certainly won't be going back there,' Maxine assured her. 'Supposing you run along to play for a few minutes while I talk to your uncle and aunt. We'll have a little talk ourselves before I go.'

Shannon concealed her own inclinations as the small chin jutted, in full sympathy with the child's reluctance to be dismissed from a conversation which had to be about her anyway. It was left to Kyle to add weight to the request with a meaningful inclination of his head.

Jodie picked up the mug of hot chocolate, not about to be robbed of that. Kyle waited until the door had closed behind her before saying levelly, 'So what exactly do you need to know?'

'Well, the factual detail we already have. We just need to be sure that you know all the pros and cons of adopting a child Jodie's age. Especially one you hadn't even met until a few days ago. According to the background detail provided by the Brisbane authorities, she was raised in a very different environment from this. She might have problems fitting in.'

'Jodie's very adaptable,' said Shannon before Kyle could answer. 'She's handled everything brilliantly up to now.'

'I'm sure she has.' The tone was soothing. 'She must think herself in heaven after what she's been used to. But it's early days yet. Things aren't always going to go smoothly. Starting a new school can be difficult for any child.'

'We'll handle whatever crops up,' Kyle asserted.

Maxine smiled and nodded. 'Let's hope for the best, anyway.' She glanced at her watch and pulled a face. 'Sorry to make it such a flying visit this time, but I'm due to see someone back at the office in half an hour. If I could just have a few words with Jodie on her own first?' She shook her head as Shannon made to get up with her, reaching for her coat. 'That's all right. Just tell me which is her room.'

'Right on the stairs, second door along the gallery,' said Kyle, already on his feet. 'We'll be seeing you again, then.'

'Yes, you will.' The girl's eyes were riveted to his face, a sudden flush staining her cheeks. 'I'm an avid reader of your books,' she declared. 'They're really excellent! You must do a tremendous amount of research.'

'A fair amount,' he agreed. 'Shannon writes too, of course.'

'I know.' She shifted her attention briefly. 'I'm afraid I can't claim to have read anything of yours. I'm more for thrillers than romance.'

Shannon gave a smiling shrug. 'That's all right. You should sign her a copy of your latest, Kyle.'

'I don't have any here,' he said, 'but I'll make sure I have one ready for your next visit.'

He went to open the door for the girl, bringing another flush to her cheeks.

'A fan worth cultivating,' Shannon commented as he closed it again.

'Can't do any harm,' he agreed lightly. 'A bit different from what I expected, I must admit.'

'Hardly your type, I'd have thought.'

The grey eyes narrowed on her face, humour fading. 'Even if she was, do you seriously think I'd be doing anything about it?'

Of course not, would have been the sensible answer, but some devil inside her wouldn't let her make it. 'Who knows?' she said instead.

Kyle drew in a long, slow breath, obviously to control too hasty a retort. 'This all stems from that phone call, doesn't it?' he stated grimly. 'You think it was Paula calling.'

'You're saying it couldn't be?'

'I've no idea who it was!'

'I suppose you've no idea what she was doing in Tonbridge on Saturday either.'

'She has friends in the area. Not mutual ones, if you're wondering.'

Shannon gazed at him, unable to govern the part of her that still suspected his word. 'You said the two of you parted by mutual agreement. Is that strictly true?'

'Does it matter?'

'To me, yes,' she said roughly.

His lips twisted. 'If you must have it, we parted for good the day I told her I'd no intention of seeking a divorce from you to marry her.'

The point at which the heroine in one of her books might have melted into the hero's arms, came the thought, but this was real life, not fiction. His not wanting to marry the woman made what he had done even worse in some respects.

'I don't imagine you've lacked female company these past months, anyway,' she said.

'You've hardly been lacking company yourself,' he pointed out. 'Or am I supposed to consider Craig in a different light?'

'*I* haven't slept with Craig.' Shannon registered the scepticism in the grey eyes without surprise; there weren't many who *would* believe it.

'You're trying to tell me he's never wanted to make love to you?'

'I didn't say that. I said—'

'You haven't slept with him.' The irony was heavy. 'That's always been a pretty ambiguous way of putting it.'

'You'd hardly expect a more explicit term from a romantic novelist, would you?' she responded with an irony of her own. 'Whether you choose to believe it or not, it's the truth.'

Kyle regarded her for a deliberating moment. 'You were planning to marry the man. You must have felt something for him.'

'I did...I do.' She hesitated, realising the trap she had fallen into, and seeing no way out of it other than to admit another truth. 'Craig's a fine man, and I have a great regard for him, but he never made me want him badly enough to go to bed with him.'

'Maybe he just didn't put enough effort into it.'

'Or maybe you were right when you suggested that you might be the only man who can turn me on that way,' she murmured, this time drawing a short laugh.

'A hold worth having, for sure!' He paused, gaze moving from her face down the slender length of her body, seemed on the verge of saying something else, then shook his head as if in rejection of whatever it was he had in mind, jaw firming. 'When were you planning on telling him?'

'As soon as possible. Only not over the phone. I have to see him.'

If she'd been honest with both Craig *and* herself yesterday, it wouldn't have been necessary, Kyle could have said, but he refrained, as always, from stating the obvious. 'Just providing it's not Wednesday.'

Shannon willed him to come over to her, if only to share a seat, but he didn't, moving back to the chair he had recently vacated and picking up the newspaper lying beside it on the floor. He knew there was no chance of her walking out on Jodie now, she thought hollowly, so he could afford to stop making too much of an effort. He wanted her when he wanted her, and this wasn't one of the times.

She was still no wiser with regard to the phone call either. While the inner London coding didn't rule out the possibility of a wrong number completely, it certainly made it less likely.

And what if it had been some woman on the line? asked the voice of reason. It couldn't be someone *au fait* with developments, which hardly suggested a close relationship. Whatever Kyle might have got up to these past eighteen months, it was time to stop harping on it and start concentrating on making their own relationship as good as possible.

'I phoned Mom earlier,' she said, rallying her spirits determinedly. 'She wants us to take Jodie over to meet them. I think she sees herself as a surrogate grandmother.'

'I'd say that's the only kind Jodie's likely to know,' Kyle observed on a dry note.

With his father somewhere in South America, and his mother remarried and living in Canada, that was probably right, Shannon realised. They'd neither of them even made the wedding.

'So how do you feel about seeing her and Dad again?' she asked after a moment.

'I dare say I can weather it. How are they, anyway?'

'Fine. Mom's over the moon!' Shannon ousted any hint of irony from her tone. 'She never lost faith in you.'

Kyle eyed her shrewdly. 'But your father might not be quite so forthcoming?'

'Initially, perhaps.'

'Then we'll have to reassure him, won't we?'

'Put on an act, you mean?'

He shrugged, expression unrevealing. 'Whatever it takes.'

Shannon studied him frustratedly as he turned his attention back to the newspaper. There had been a time when she would have gone to him, taken the paper from his hands and teased him into making love to her. She'd only had to look at him to want him. She felt the same way now, her insides turning liquid at the memory of last night's excesses. He'd been so passionate, so excitingly assertive. In his arms she could forget everything.

'You must be itching to get back to work,' she said, only just resisting the temptation to follow through on her inclinations. 'Jodie and I will be fine if you want to make a start.'

'Hardly worthwhile if I have to break off again,' he returned without looking up. 'Once she's settled in school we'll both be free to get to work.'

Shannon hadn't got round to considering that aspect as yet. The three books she'd written during the fourteen months they'd lived together had been done on a typewriter, which was probably still here, but she was accustomed now to using a word processor.

'I'll need to see about getting my stuff over from the flat first,' she observed. 'It might be an idea to convert the small bedroom at the back to a study for me, don't you think, instead of me working in here the way I used to?'

This time the dark head lifted, his regard enigmatic. 'You're giving up the flat?'

'If I'm going to be here, I'm hardly going to need it.'

There was a pause that seemed to last for minutes while he continued to study her. Her heart rate soared when he put the newspaper aside and got purposefully to his feet. Drawn up and into his arms, she responded without restraint, feeling the pressure building inside her as he kissed her, wanting him, loving him—desperate to be convinced that he wasn't just using her.

The opening of the door brought things to a halt, although Kyle didn't let go of her, not in the least discomfited as he looked at the girl framed in the doorway.

'I'm so sorry!' Maxine apologised. 'I just came to tell

you Jodie and I were finished, and to say goodbye for now. I should have knocked.'

'No problem,' Kyle assured her. 'I dare say you've seen husbands and wives kissing before.'

'Not that often in my line,' she admitted. 'Rowing, yes. It makes a nice change.' The glance she gave Shannon held not a little envy. 'See you both next week, then.'

Shannon detached herself from the arm about her shoulders, trying not to give too much credence to a suspicion that the whole scene had been set up to impress the social worker with their marital harmony. He would have to have heard the girl coming down the stairs, which seemed unlikely given the thickness of the door.

'I'll see you out,' she said.

She waited until they were out in the hall before asking how things had gone with Jodie, wondering why the child hadn't come down herself yet.

Maxine gave a wry smile. 'Not very communicative, is she? I did manage to get out of her that she hates school, which isn't very encouraging. I don't suppose you've had time to think about it yet, but you'll need to be getting her in somewhere before too long.'

'We've an appointment with the principal at Silverwood on Wednesday,' Shannon advised reluctantly, unsurprised to see a doubtful expression cross the other girl's face.

'Considering her particular background, a private school might not be the most suitable choice.'

That had been her own opinion only a couple of days ago, Shannon reminded herself, curbing the instinctive retort. It was still, if she was honest about it. Jodie's intelligence wasn't in doubt, but there was every chance that she'd be way out of her depth at Silverwood, academically *and* socially. Children could be cruel when it came to anyone who was in any way different, and Jodie's accent alone would make her that. If she dealt with taunters the same way she had dealt with Robby back at the home, all hell would break loose.

'You'll have to talk to my husband about that,' she said, regretting it the moment the words left her mouth.

Maxine gave her a sharpened glance. 'You've different views in that direction, then?'

'I just meant it would be better discussing it together, that's all.' As retrievals went it left a lot to be desired, but it was the best Shannon could do. For the next thirteen weeks at least, it was necessary that she and Kyle appear to be in accord on every aspect of Jodie's welfare.

Whether Maxine believed her or not, she made no further comment. It could be no more than a minor detail in this report of hers, anyway, Shannon assured herself, closing the door. The ultimate decision would be based on far more pertinent factors than a difference of opinion over schools.

About to return to the morning room, she paused as her eye caught a movement at the head of the stairs.

'Coming down again?' she called, when the small figure made no further move.

There was no answer. Shannon hesitated a moment, uncertain of the best approach, then followed her instincts and made her way up to the child sitting on the top step.

'What's wrong?' she asked gently, taking a seat beside her.

'She said it's going to be weeks and weeks before I can be adopted.' Both expression and tone were unusually subdued.

'That's just to make sure you're happy and properly

cared for,' Shannon assured her, achieving no visible lifting of restraint.

'She said I'll have to go to court and see a judge.'

'We'll all be going. It's just a formality. There's nothing to worry about, honestly. You're here for good.'

Jodie digested that in silence for a moment before bursting out aggrievedly, 'She said I've got to go to school too!'

'Well…yes.' Shannon made every effort to keep a straight face, recognising the real source of despondency. 'It's the law here the same as it was back home. Don't you like school?'

'It's boring!'

'It might be better at a new one.' Not exactly an inspiring comment, Shannon acknowledged wryly. 'You must have realised you can't not go to school at all.'

Jodie pulled a fierce face. 'I wish I was grown-up, then I wouldn't have to do *anything* I didn't want to!'

'Grown-ups have to do things they don't like doing too.'

'Dad never did anything *he* didn't want to do! He said rules were for fools.'

It was going to take a long time, Shannon reflected wrathfully, to expunge the harm that man had done!

'Grown-ups aren't always right either,' she said with care. 'We all say silly things at times.' Do them too, came the mental rider. 'Anyway,' she added, 'you'll not be going this week, so let's make the most of it. How would you like to get wrapped up and go for a good long walk in the snow this afternoon? There's a nice little café in the village where we could have tea.'

The gamine features brightened a little. 'Uncle Kyle too?'

'Supposing you go and ask him. I have to make a

phone call. We'll be going to visit my parents tomorrow. They're looking forward to meeting you.'

There was a sudden and reassuring hint of mischief in the grey eyes. 'I suppose you'll want me to be on my best behaviour, then.'

Shannon grinned back, relieved by the return to normality. 'I'll settle for the basic model.'

She made the call from the study, seated at the wide oak desk. Kyle's computer and printer were on a side desk, with the castored swivel chair convenient to both. A leather-bound set of Encyclopedia Britannica occupied a prime position on the bookshelves lining the room. Her present to him, the one Christmas they had spent together, Shannon recalled with a pang. Somewhat redundant these days, she supposed, with the Internet able to provide detailed information on just about every subject under the sun, but no less impressive to look at. He'd seemed pleased enough with them, at any rate.

That had been before things started falling apart, of course. At least so far as she had been aware at the time. Looking back now, she suspected that the rot had set in even then.

A waste of time going over it all again, anyway. She had enough on her plate dealing with the present.

Delighted to hear they would be making the trip so soon, her mother attempted to persuade her to spend a night there so that they could all relax with a drink in the evening. Shannon used the visit they were scheduled to make to Silverwood on the Wednesday as an excuse, doubting, in any case, if Kyle would have been prepared to stay overnight. Brenton was hardly far enough away to make it necessary, she could hear him saying.

About to vacate the chair after ringing off, she hesitated, eyes on the left-hand top drawer of the work desk, where Kyle always kept printed copy when he was writing. She hated anyone reading her own partially completed manuscripts, but the urge now to sneak a look at his was irresistible.

She had made a point of not reading his last publication because she hadn't been able to bear the thought that he'd written it while he was with Paula. Not that the woman would have had a hand in it, of course, but the knowledge that they'd been seeing one another at the time was enough. If the affair really had been over for months, then this new one had no such taint. Just the first page, perhaps...

She slid the chair smoothly across and opened the drawer, to sit for several moments gazing with darkened eyes at the gold hoop earring lying on top of the stacked copy. Not hers, for certain, so whose? And why here?

Because it had been lost right here, perhaps. Kyle made love where and when he felt like it, and the sofa over there was as handy as anywhere else in the house. She could visualise him picking up the earring later, weighing it in his hand with that reminiscent smile, then putting it in his work drawer where Mrs Parkin wouldn't be likely to see it until he could safely return it.

Except that he hadn't had the opportunity to return it because this thing with Jodie had come up and he'd found it necessary to bring her, Shannon, back into the picture. Not that having a wife around again need be any detriment.

She closed the drawer again and rolled the chair back to its original place, sitting there for a moment or two gazing unseeingly at the tooled leather surface as she grappled with her thoughts. Confronting Kyle with the earring would mean admitting that she'd been ferreting around in his desk, and that she wasn't prepared to do. Building a whole scenario around a simple piece of jewellery was ridiculous, anyway; there could be a perfectly innocent explanation.

And pigs might fly! scoffed that inner voice.

CHAPTER NINE

WHATEVER Neville Holroyd's reservations, he made no great show of them when greeting his son-in-law. Both he and his wife were captivated by Jodie, who within minutes of arrival made herself totally at home.

'She's a delightful child!' Lucy declared when she and Shannon went to set the dining-room table for lunch. 'It says a lot for Kyle that he was willing to take on a nine-year-old at his age, even if she is his niece. You too, of course,' she added, casting her daughter a fond glance. 'It's amazing how well you've all of you adjusted in such a short time. Just to think that this time last month you and Kyle were separated, and now here you are together again, and with a child to care for too!' She paused. 'You won't let it put you off having one of your own, though, will you?'

'There's plenty of time to think about that,' Shannon said lightly. 'Women have babies in their forties these days.'

'They may very well do, but I hope *you'll* not think of leaving it that long! You have to remember that Kyle's ten years older than you are. I can't see any man taking too well to sleepless nights in his fifties!'

Shannon couldn't imagine Kyle in his fifties at all— nor herself in her forties, if it came to that. They were together now only because of Jodie. By the time she was old enough to fend for herself, would there be anything left to stay together for?

'I'll bear it in mind,' she murmured.

'Well, at least you got yourselves sorted out, though

why it had to take something like this to make you both see sense I don't know! Anyway, all's well that ends well. Oh, not those place mats, darling! We'll use the new ones Aunt Muriel bought me for Christmas.'

One thing about her mother, Shannon thought gratefully—her comments rarely required specific responses. She would have lost little time in spreading the news that her daughter and husband had resolved their problems at last, and was hell-bent now on what she saw as the next logical step. It wasn't even beyond her to start knitting baby clothes in the hope of sparking some latent desire—though she could knit a whole layette for all the difference it would make. Unless Kyle could convince her that he was going to stay faithful this time round, her mother would just have to yearn.

The two men were talking together without apparent constraint when she went to call them through for lunch. On her knees playing with the family cat, Jodie put up no resistance when told to go and wash her hands before they ate, although she had intimated more than once that she saw it as a complete waste of time and effort when they weren't even dirty in her estimation. Shannon could only hope for the same co-operation when it came to outside authority.

She had broached the schools question with Kyle again last night, but she hadn't got anywhere. The principal had already been advised of the position, and had no qualms about taking Jodie on, he'd said. Children learned by example, so a well-disciplined regime such as Silverwood could guarantee to supply was exactly what was needed.

Trust him or not, she'd still been unable to resist him when he'd reached for her. What that made her she wasn't sure. A hypocrite came close.

Her father waited until they were alone for a few

minutes before expressing any disquiet over the marriage renewal.

'You're quite sure you're doing the right thing?' he asked tentatively. 'I can see how you feel about Jodie already, but it's your life too. I'd hate to see you hurt again.'

'I shan't be,' Shannon assured him, wishing she could feel as confident as she sounded. 'It's different this time.'

He gave a faint smile. 'Is it? I like Kyle, but a man as attractive to women as he is will always have a lot of temptation put his way.'

'Then I'll just have to bolster his resistance, won't I?' she said. 'Perhaps if I'd made an effort to fight for him instead of just taking off the way I did we might never have parted in the first place.'

'You said he wasn't worth fighting for at the time.'

'Only because I was trying to convince myself that I was well out of it anyway.' Shannon lifted her shoulders in a wry little shrug. 'I was living out a fantasy when I married him. I didn't realise that marriage needs working at.'

'Few do,' her father commented. 'But if Jodie is the only reason the two of you are trying again it won't work any better than it did last time.'

It wasn't *her* only reason, she could have told him, but she couldn't vouch for Kyle. One thing was certain: she wouldn't be walking away again, however things turned out. Jodie had to take priority.

They left at four, with Lucy's exhortations to come again soon ringing in their ears.

'Are we eating out tonight?' asked Jodie plaintively from the rear of the car, when they were on the motorway.

'You can't possibly be hungry again after what you ate at lunch!' Shannon protested.

'I am,' she claimed. 'I'm a growing girl!'

'Up, or out?' teased Kyle. 'We'll stop off at the next services and get you a snack to be going on with.'

Shannon opened her mouth to remonstrate, then closed it again. The child had known few enough indulgences in her short life; a few extra calories were hardly going to do her any harm.

Reluctant to sit in the car on her own, she accompanied the two of them into the brightly lit warmth of the central unit, leaving them discussing the rival merits of several different types of chocolate bar while she drifted across to look at the book stand.

There were none of hers on the rack, but a single copy of Kyle's latest caught her eye. It was quite ridiculous to buy it when he could so easily get hold of a copy for her, yet she did it anyway, tucking it out of sight in her capacious shoulder bag as she waited for her change. If the leading female character turned out to be a sultry brunette, she could always bin it.

'Your little girl is very like her daddy, isn't she?' remarked the middle-aged woman at the till with a friendly smile. 'A real live wire, too, I'll bet!' Her smile widened as the two of them came up at Shannon's back. 'Chocolate, is it? You'll have your teeth dropping out!'

'I'll have some false ones, then.' Jodie deposited three bars on the counter, beaming up at the woman. 'One for now and two for later.'

'*Much* later,' appended Kyle drily. 'That's to last you all week.'

The contrast between Australian accent and educated English, combined with the marked resemblance between man and child, brought a sudden confusion to the woman's kindly face. Shannon briefly contemplated explaining the relationship, but decided that Kyle might not appreciate the gesture.

'She thought you were her natural father,' she said as they left the shop, with Jodie skipping on ahead. 'I hadn't realised myself just how much alike the two of you really do look until just now.'

'Janine and I were very much alike,' Kyle acknowledged.

He slid an unexpected arm about her shoulders, drawing her closer as they walked, his lean muscularity a stimulant in itself. For a moment, Shannon could almost believe they were back where they'd started—although she'd doubted the depth of his feelings for her even then, she remembered.

She caught a glimpse of the two of them in a mirrored inset at the centre entrance: Kyle so tall and dark in the cashmere overcoat, her head no higher than his jawline, hair catching the light as it fell softly about her face— the way he had always liked her to wear it in the past.

They looked good together, she thought, feeling the impact on her stomach muscles as she stole another glance at the incisive profile. They were going to stay together too. This time, for better or for worse had to mean something.

They got home to find that Mrs Parkin had left another of her casseroles in the oven, which at least solved the problem of where they were going to eat. Lunch and chocolate notwithstanding, Jodie ate everything put before her, and asked for seconds.

'I like your mom and dad,' she declared, helping Shannon load the dishwasher afterwards. 'Your mom said I could call them Nana and Grandpa, but that will only be if I get adopted, won't it?'

'There's no "if" about it,' Shannon returned swiftly, alert to the plea for reassurance. 'This waiting period is just something we have to go through to assure the authorities that we're all of us happy to be together.'

Jodie gave her a contemplative glance. 'Are you and Uncle Kyle happy to be together?'

The question tied Shannon's tongue in knots for a moment or two. Casting her mind back over the past few days, she could remember no incident that might have suggested a rift—not in Jodie's company, at any rate.

'Of course,' she said, trying not to over-emphasise. 'Very happy.'

The answer appeared to satisfy, although there was no knowing for certain what was going on inside the small dark head. She had a whole lot more of Kyle in her than just looks, thought Shannon wryly, closing the dishwasher door.

Kyle had switched on the television for the evening news, and was idly watching some poor soul on a panel being put through the hoop by a sadistically smiling quizmaster when the two of them returned to the sitting room.

'What is seventy-one multiplied by a hundred and thirty-one?' the latter was asking as the two of them came in.

'Nine thousand, three hundred and one,' said Jodie a whole second before a competitor came up with the same answer.

Dumbfounded, Shannon looked across at Kyle, to see him regarding his niece with equal astonishment.

'Did you find that easy?' he asked.

Jodie shrugged. 'It wasn't very hard.'

'Supposing you try some more?' he suggested on a casual note. 'Just to see how quick you are?'

The grey eyes so like his own registered a faint interest. 'Okay.'

She beat the competitors on the next half-dozen problems, stumped only when the figures went to five places.

Shannon could hardly believe it. This was a nine-year-old, for heaven's sake!

'Your mother was good with numbers too,' Kyle commented lightly when he finally called a halt. 'She used to say how boring it was at school because everyone else was so slow. Is that how you feel too?'

The shrug was repeated, the sparkle acquired over the last few minutes fading a little. 'I guess.'

'Well, I don't think you'll be bored at your new one.'

Jodie made no reply to that, but she looked unconvinced. She was subdued for the rest of the evening, going off to bed at nine without even being told.

'Surely someone must have realised what she was capable of before this,' Shannon remarked as the door closed in her wake.

Kyle gave a brief shrug. 'Depends whether she let anyone know. She's astute enough to realise it makes her different, and any child who's different gets picked on by others. Janine found it difficult enough, and she was nowhere near as quick.'

'It's possible she's a whole lot better reader than I've been giving her credit for too,' Shannon said thoughtfully. 'Those books we bought her probably aren't advanced enough to hold her attention for long. We might even have an all-round prodigy on our hands!'

'They'll sort her out at Silverwood.' If Kyle was feeling vindicated, he wasn't showing it. 'Did you get in touch with Craig yet?'

'Not personally,' she admitted, thrown for a moment by the sudden change of subject. 'I left a message on his answering machine.'

'To what effect?'

'I told him I couldn't make Wednesday, and said I'd see him the same place on Thursday.'

'Supposing *he* can't make it?'

'He'd have phoned back by now.' Shannon directed a terse glance at him. 'If you're thinking of saying I should tell him over the phone, forget it!'

'As a matter of fact, I was thinking we might spend a couple of days at the apartment. I could drive up separately with Jodie and meet you there Thursday evening, then take her round the sights together Friday.' The strong mouth slanted. 'It's what families do.'

He really was making every effort, Shannon conceded. Jodie, she was sure, would love it.

'It sounds a good idea,' she said, wishing she didn't have Craig to face first. 'I can go and collect some more clothes from the flat, then come straight to the apartment.'

'That's settled, then.' There was a pause, the grey eyes acquiring an expression that set her pulses racing. 'Come over here,' he invited softly.

'I'm not in the mood,' she returned, giving way to a flash of resentment at his assumption that all he had to do was beckon. 'Anyway, Jodie might come down again.'

'I wasn't suggesting an orgy. Still...' he lifted a philosophical shoulder '...if you're not in the mood for a kiss and a cuddle, you're not in the mood. I'll just have to settle for more television instead.'

Shannon bit her lip as he used the remote control to switch the set on and settled back comfortably in his seat. What little satisfaction she had gained from refusing his invitation was more than outweighed by the realisation that he didn't consider the matter worth pursuing. But then, why would he bother when there were plenty of others out there only too willing to gratify his desires?

Later, in bed, she turned her back on him, torn between conflicting emotions when he slid an arm about her waist to draw her close against him.

'Keep wriggling like that and I can't guarantee not to react,' he murmured against her ear as she attempted to break his hold on her.

'So let go of me!' she hissed, and heard his low laugh.

'You don't really want that.'

It was true, she didn't. The muscular warmth at her back was enough to undermine any resolution. Shannon stopped struggling, closing her eyes as he moved his hand up to seek her breast, feeling the heat beginning to radiate through her body.

'Better,' Kyle said softly. 'Much, much better!' He turned her over onto her back, supporting himself on an elbow to look down at her in the darkness, his free hand gliding slowly over the smooth satin of her nightdress to find the hem. 'Now what was all that about?'

Ask him about the earring, urged that inner voice. At least see what story he comes up with. Only there were other, far stronger urgings rising in her as that questing hand slid caressingly up the inner side of her calf.

'I just don't like being taken for granted,' she got out huskily.

With no moonlight tonight, it was impossible to see the expression in his eyes, but there was no mistaking the amusement in his smile.

'Is that what I'm doing?'

What he was doing was driving her out of her mind with that lighter-than-light fingertip stroking from ankle to knee and back again. She stirred restlessly, thighs parting involuntarily as he lengthened the stroke, exposing the soft inner skin to his touch.

He put his lips very gently to hers, easing his tongue between them to rim the very edge of her teeth before exploring deeper. She was drowned in sensation, body opening to him, hands seeking his hardness and drawing him to her in hungry impatience, hearing him laugh exultantly as he came over her. He penetrated deeply, possessively, holding for a moment to press his lips to her temple before starting to move—building the pace until they could neither of them hold out any longer.

When it came to mind over matter, she was fighting a losing battle, Shannon acknowledged ruefully when she could think again at all. Kyle had her hog-tied, and he knew it.

The meeting with Craig proved just as difficult as anticipated.

'You must have known you were going to do this on Sunday,' he accused with justifiable bitterness. 'Why didn't you tell me then?'

Shannon made a wry gesture. 'I was still trying to make myself believe I could walk away from it all, I suppose. I'm sorry, Craig. Really and truly sorry.'

'You'll be sorrier still when that husband of yours goes on the make again,' he said hardily. 'He's using you, Shannon. If he'd wanted to try again, he'd have done something about it before this.'

It was what she had told herself more than once, and the last thing she needed reminding of right now. She forced a smile, a light shrug. 'Maybe he needed an excuse, male pride being what it is.'

'You think it's just *my* pride that's suffering?' Craig retorted. 'I'd never have asked you to marry me if I hadn't loved you!'

Past tense, Shannon noted. Not that she could blame him. 'There's nothing I can say except I'm sorry,' she repeated doggedly, knowing it was totally inadequate.

She attempted to mitigate the guilt on leaving him by assuring herself that he'd soon find someone else. Craig had a lot going for him—more than enough for most women. If she'd never known Kyle, it would more than likely have been enough for her.

Not that she really knew Kyle now, she supposed—except in the biblical sense. She felt the familiar frisson run down her spinal column as his image formed in her mind's eye: the ripple of muscle beneath tanned skin, the mat of dark hair covering his chest, the strong thighs and virile manhood. As a lover, he was everything she had ever imagined or could ever want. Many women would be happy to settle for *that* much.

The sight of a traffic warden a few cars down the parked line, coupled with the realisation that the meter she was parked on was already into the red, drove everything else from her mind for the moment.

She made it away by the skin of her teeth, forcing an entry into the moving traffic and signalling a tongue-in-cheek thanks to the furiously gesticulating male in the blue BMW. Driving something as big as the Range Rover certainly had its advantages.

Having already decided to let the agency she had bought the flat through handle the resale for her, she got on the phone as soon as she arrived and arranged to drop in a set of keys. With regard to the furnishings there were a few minor items she would want to keep, but the rest would have to be disposed of one way or another. For now, she was only interested in obtaining some more clothes.

She exchanged the red trouser suit for a figure-fitting green jersey dress before she started packing the two suitcases, laying aside a long suede coat to wear over it. She was still only halfway through when the phone rang. Writing having been far from her thoughts recently, it came as something of a surprise to hear her editor's voice.

'I've been trying to get hold of you for ages!' Barbara exclaimed. 'I even tried ringing the house last week.'

'What made you think I might be there anyway?' Shannon asked cautiously.

'The fact that Kyle was looking for you a couple of weeks back.' The pause was rife with curiosity. 'Did he find you?'

Over the years, Barbara had become a friend as well as an advisor, the decade or so difference in ages no detriment. Shannon saw no point in trying to keep her altered circumstances a secret—especially as she wasn't going to be spending any more time at this address.

'He not only found me,' she said, 'he persuaded me to give it another go.'

Barbara kept the response low-key, apparently not quite certain whether congratulations were in order. 'And how is it going?'

'Fine. Just fine!'

'Really?' The scepticism came across loud and clear.

'Really,' Shannon assured her, crossing her fingers. Now was the time to mention Jodie, but she couldn't bring herself to do it. 'A few teething problems,' she said instead, 'but we're ironing them out.'

'You always did like mixing your metaphors.' It was obvious from the dry tone that Barbara wasn't wholly convinced. 'Good luck with it, anyway.' She briskened to add, 'When are you planning on getting back to work?'

'Soon,' Shannon promised, with very little idea of how soon that might be.

'Just providing you don't leave it too long. You know how fickle readers can be.' She paused again. 'You'll not be giving up the flat just yet?'

'Yes, I shall.'

Barbara made no verbal comment, though her opinion

came across loud and clear: what had happened once could quite well happen again. But then, she didn't know about Jodie.

'How about lunch next week?' she suggested. 'I can do Tuesday.'

'I'm not sure,' Shannon hedged. 'Can I let you know?'

'Fine. I'll pencil it in anyway. Twelve-thirty at Lockets, unless I hear otherwise.'

Shannon replaced the receiver, standing there for a moment or two considering. Barbara was right, of course; she needed to get back to work—if only to retain some financial independence. With Jodie in school, there would be nothing to stop her from following her normal working routine.

After yesterday's session with the Silverwood principal, she felt a great deal more confidence, she had to admit. Children with higher intelligence often resorted to belligerence out of sheer frustration when they weren't stretched, he'd said, after despatching Jodie to look round the school with a pupil not much older than she was. She would soon settle down.

Jodie herself had grudgingly conceded on the way home that it might not be too bad, after all.

There was plenty of room in the Range Rover for her computer and other equipment, so she might as well take it now, Shannon decided, coming back to the present. She had insisted that Kyle have the study when they'd first moved into the house, and had been quite happy to use the morning room herself, but it was a far better idea to have one of the spare bedrooms converted this time. Professional fitters shouldn't take long to do the job.

By the time she'd made the detour to drop off the keys at the agency, the early evening traffic was building fast. It was gone five-thirty when she finally reached the Dockside apartment block.

Not that she need have worried, as neither Kyle nor Jodie was at the apartment, just a note saying they'd gone to the Planetarium and would be back around six.

The first time Shannon had seen the suite of rooms Kyle called home she had found the whole place too overtly masculine in its preponderance of leather and wood, no matter how luxurious the effect. A change of drapes and a few flower arrangements were the only touches he had allowed her here, although he'd given her free rein with the house.

The glass doors forming almost the entire wall of the vast living room framed a magnificent view over the river. She spent a whole five minutes gazing out at it, remembering the good times. Or had they only been good for her? Had Kyle realised from the start that he'd made a mistake in marrying her?

Useless speculation, she thought hollowly, pulling herself away to go and make a cup of coffee in the superbly designed and equipped kitchen.

It was only on returning to the living room that she saw the red light on the answering machine. There were two messages. After only a moment's hesitation, Shannon rewound the tape and pressed playback.

'I often wonder why you bother with a mobile at all when it's switched off half the time,' declared a female voice without preamble. 'I tried to reach you at the house. Your cleaning lady said you'd come up to town.' There was a brief pause, a change of tone. 'It's con-firmed, darling! This morning. I know you have other matters on your mind right now, but we have to deal with this together. I'll be waiting to hear from you.'

The second caller hadn't spoken. Shannon stood im-mobile as the machine reset, mind in turmoil. There was only one interpretation she could think of to put on that announcement: this woman, whoever she might be, was carrying Kyle's child!

CHAPTER TEN

IT WAS gone six-thirty when the missing two finally arrived, Jodie bubbling over with enthusiasm for the Planetarium and Madame Tussaud's, both of which they'd managed to fit into the afternoon.

'Sorry we were so long,' proffered Kyle when he could get a word in edgeways. 'Getting a taxi this time of day is nearly as hard as finding a parking space. We could almost have walked it in the time!'

'I wanted to go on the underground,' said Jodie, 'but there were too many people. Uncle Kyle says we can go to the zoo on it tomorrow. You'll come too, won't you?'

'Of course.' Shannon did her best to sound suitably enthused, aware that her best wasn't good enough when Kyle gave her a suddenly sharpened glance.

'I thought we might try one of the local bistros tonight,' he said. 'Any preferences?'

'What's a bistro?' asked Jodie, busy experimenting with one of the reclining chairs.

'Just a small restaurant,' Shannon supplied. 'I don't mind where we go,' she tagged on for Kyle's benefit, wondering bleakly if this other woman could cook as well as conceive.

He shrugged. 'I'll go and get a quick shower, then. I like the dress, by the way,' he added in passing.

'I changed at the flat,' she said for no particular reason, and saw his mouth take on a slant.

'Saves time, I suppose. Give me fifteen minutes. I need a shave.'

'I don't need to get washed and changed again too,

165

do I?' asked Jodie hopefully. 'I haven't been anywhere to get dirty.'

Shannon gave her a cursory inspection. The smart brown cords and matching jacket she was wearing showed no marks that she could see, and the small face certainly looked clean enough. Her tan had already faded a little, she noted, although it was unlikely that it would go completely. Jodie had the same naturally bronzed skin as Kyle, as had her mother too, no doubt.

Kyle. What she was going to do about this new development she had no real idea as yet. The message had been wiped from the machine, but there was no wiping out the knowledge that somewhere out there was a woman waiting to hear from the man whose child she was carrying.

From the tone of the message, he had to be aware that the possibility existed—though surely by accident, not design? Whichever, if the woman went ahead and had the child, he would be responsible for its welfare, and considering the way he felt about Jodie, who wasn't even his own child, it wouldn't be just a financial interest either.

If she had given him a child herself when he'd wanted it—or at the very least attempted to—everything might have been different. Only now, after seeing the way he was with Jodie, could she appreciate his desire for the kind of family life he had missed out on himself due to his warring parents.

Jodie was still waiting for an answer, Shannon realised at that point.

'You'll do,' she said.

Grey eyes regarded her speculatively. 'If you're upset because we went to the Planetarium without you, we could go again tomorrow. I don't mind missing the zoo. Well…not much, anyway.'

Shannon had to smile. 'I'm not upset. In any case, I've seen the Planetarium before, and I haven't been to a zoo for years.'

'That's all right, then.' The relief came through loud and clear. 'I've never been on a train under the ground!'

It was doubtful if she'd ever been on a train at all, thought Shannon, and came to a decision. Unless there was further contact from this woman between times, the confrontation could wait until they got back to the house. In the meantime, she had to try and carry on as normal.

Kyle emerged clean-shaven and immaculate in a dark grey suit worn casually over a fine pale blue sweater. Watching him as he checked that he had his wallet, Shannon doubted if there would ever come a time when she could view his lithe length without her heart dancing a fandango. Even now, knowing what she did, she still wanted him desperately.

For a moment the grey eyes met hers, dark and impenetrable. It was Shannon who looked away, unable to sustain the contact.

'Let's go,' she said briefly.

He and Jodie kept a lively conversation going throughout the meal. They were more like father and daughter already than uncle and niece, Shannon reflected, listening to the two of them. One thing she was certain of: Kyle wouldn't abandon the child, no matter what.

Feeling the way she did, she could empathise with Craig. There was a man who had truly loved her—who probably still did love her, even after she had kicked him in the teeth. A good man, who would have devoted his life to her happiness had she given him the chance. Not that he wasn't better off without her. He deserved far more than she could ever have given him in the way of love.

There was no further message on the answering machine when they got back to the apartment. Jodie asked if she could have the television on, which at least passed another hour, although Shannon couldn't afterwards have said what the programme they had watched was about. She could feel Kyle's eyes on her from time to time, but she steadfastly refused to glance in his direction.

His suggestion that it was time a certain person retired to bed drew a heartfelt protest. She wasn't in the least bit tired yet, and wouldn't be able to sleep, Jodie claimed, making no impression at all on her smiling but adamant uncle.

'Drink?' he asked after the small, resigned figure had finally departed for the guest room.

About to refuse, Shannon abruptly changed her mind. Alcohol at least blunted the edges. 'I wouldn't mind a gin and lime,' she said.

Already at the cabinet, Kyle shook his head. 'Sorry, we're out of lime juice. How about tonic?'

'Fine.'

He brought the drinks across, regaining his seat to look at her with lifted brows. 'Going to tell me what's bugging you?'

As openings went, she wasn't going to get a better one, but she couldn't bring herself to take advantage of it. 'What makes you think anything's bugging me?' she asked lightly.

'The fact that you've hardly had a word to say for yourself all evening, for one thing.'

'Silence is golden,' she quipped, giving rise to an impatient exclamation.

'Stop prevaricating. It's obvious you've *something* on your mind!'

Short of flinging the whole thing in his face here and

now, which she still hesitated to do, there was only one way out she could think of on the spur of the moment—and not so much of a lie.

'It's just that time of the month. One of the crosses we women have to bear.'

'I won't ask what the others are.' Kyle paused, eyes acquiring a silvery glint as they roved her slender curves. 'I know a very good way to relieve tension.'

Right now, he was going all out to heighten it. For a moment Shannon was tempted to shut her mind to everything else but the moment. Instead, she heard herself saying coolly, 'As I just told you, it's the wrong time of the month.'

'I was under the impression that the P in PMT meant prior to the event, not during.'

'What would a man know about PMT?' she flashed.

He gave a dry smile. 'The amount of publicity it gets these days, we're all pretty well up on it. Why don't you be honest and just say no? I've told you before, it isn't mandatory.'

Sitting there, so dark and vital, he was wreaking havoc on her emotions. Shannon touched the tip of her tongue to parched lips, trying to be realistic. She wouldn't be walking out on this marriage again while Jodie was a part of it, so it came down to a straight choice. Either she lived like a nun for the duration, or she accepted things the way they were and took it from there.

'Wasn't it you who said actions spoke louder than words?' she asked huskily.

The firm mouth took on a sardonic tilt. 'It works both ways.'

Meaning *he* wasn't going to be doing the showing this time, she gathered. Her first instinct was to tell him to go to hell—except that her motor responses appeared to be on autopilot.

Kyle didn't move as she crossed the few feet of carpet between them to rest both hands on the chair-back at either side of the dark head and put her lips to his. She heard him murmur something deep in his throat, then his hands were on her hips, drawing her down to him, his mouth hungry as always.

They made it to the bedroom, locking the door against possible intrusion. Kyle switched off the lamps and opened the drapes to admit the silvery moonlight, shedding his clothing as he came back to where Shannon lay waiting for him, magnificent in his nudity.

The green dress slid off easily, filmy underwear yielding without a struggle. She welcomed him with open arms and ready lips when he lowered himself to her, running her hands down the length of his back as they came together to cup the firm male hemispheres and hold him deep inside her for a long, pulsing moment—seeing his eyes fire.

Whatever he'd done, however he really felt about her, she loved this man, she told herself fiercely. She would fight to her last breath before she gave up on him again!

That was her last coherent thought as she followed him blindly, sensually, wantonly into exquisite oblivion.

Jodie was fascinated by the underground, and would happily have spent the entire day down there if the zoo hadn't exerted an even greater pull. The blasé act was largely forgotten as she zoomed between the various enclosures. Where other children seemed to be content enough just looking, she wanted to know everything there was to be known about every animal and bird she came across, collaring any keeper who came within range.

'I've a feeling we're going to have our work cut out keeping up with her once she really gets into her stride,'

commented Kyle amusedly, watching the animated little
face as she put yet another attendant through his paces.
'I found her in the study looking through Britannica A
to Bib the other morning. We'll start her off with a junior
encyclopedia set tomorrow in Tonbridge when we go to
get her fitted out for school.'

'Does that mean we'll be going back tonight?' asked
Shannon after a moment.

'Not necessarily. We can leave in the morning after
breakfast, and go straight there. Lucky the girls are allowed to wear trousers in winter. That gives you a couple of months to break down the barrier against skirts.'
He grinned at her expression. 'I'm hardly qualified myself.'

She knew what he *was* qualified for, she thought as
he turned his attention back to the child again. Too well
did she know!

'I think it might be best if we did go back tonight,'
she said. 'Otherwise, it means taking both cars into
Tonbridge. I've a load of stuff in the Rover too.'

'So I saw.' He sounded easy. 'Fair enough. I'll phone
Mrs Parkin and ask her to leave us something ready for
dinner.'

'Let me,' Shannon offered quickly as he took the
small mobile telephone from his jacket pocket, remembering that the tape message had mentioned phoning the
house first, and afraid that Mrs Parkin might refer to the
call. 'You go and rescue that keeper.'

She moved to a nearby seat to dial the number, feeling
a total hypocrite as she watched him stroll across to join
Jodie at the elephant enclosure. She had lain awake for
an age last night while he'd slept at her side, trying to
pluck up the courage to wake him and tell him what she
knew. If this woman didn't hear from him soon she

would obviously contact him again, so what use was there in keeping it from him?

Mrs Parkin answered the call almost immediately. She was standing right beside the phone in the study, she said when Shannon commented on the speed.

'How about if I pop down to the village and get some steak and kidney for a pie?' she suggested readily when the request was put to her. 'I can leave it all ready to cook. The vegetables too.' She paused. 'There was a call for Mr Beaumont yesterday, by the way. I hope I did right in saying where he'd gone? I mean, it did sound *very* urgent.'

Shannon reassured her, wondering if the woman had hazarded a shrewd guess as to the reason for that urgency. She might even know who the caller was.

'Okay?' asked Kyle as she pushed down the aerial, startling her because she hadn't seen the two of them approaching.

'Fine.' She summoned a smile. 'How does steak and kidney pie sound?'

'Like a very good idea.' There was a thoughtful look in the grey eyes as he viewed her. 'Had enough, have you?'

With Jodie looking suddenly anxious at the possibility of having the day curtailed, there was only one answer Shannon could bring herself to give. 'Of course not,' she said brightly. 'We didn't see the reptile house yet.'

It was gone three when they finally left the zoo, and the Friday evening rush was already getting under way on the underground. Having figured out the system on the way up, Jodie led the way unerringly when they changed lines.

'S'easy,' she claimed when Shannon confessed to still being prone to confusion at times. 'We need the Circle line now, see, going east. All you have to do is follow the signs.' She gave a sigh of sheer bliss. 'I love London!'

'Seems we might be spending more than one weekend in town,' commented Kyle as they followed the small figure onto the platform. 'She has a whole programme mapped out.'

He was going to have more to think about than sight-seeing trips, Shannon reflected. A whole lot more! She would have to face him with it at some point soon; the knowledge was eating her up.

'When were you planning on getting back to work?' she asked when they were on the train.

'Monday,' he said. 'Providing nothing crops up to stop me.'

'Are you expecting anything to crop up?'

'There's always a chance.' Kyle gave her a swift glance, dark brows drawn together a fraction. 'Why?'

'Three more stops!' announced Jodie, eyes on the route map displayed on the opposite bulkhead.

'Four,' Kyle corrected, glancing up at the map himself.

'I meant after this one, of course,' came the ready rejoinder as the train slid into a station.

He grinned. 'I should have known that.'

Shannon was relieved when he appeared to have forgotten the foregoing conversation. Much as she needed to get things off her chest, this was neither the time nor the place. Later, when they were back at the house and Jodie was in bed, would be the time to start getting to grips with the matter.

By the time they reached the apartment it was already too late to beat the main traffic congestion out of the city. Kyle proposed waiting until after seven when things would have calmed down a little.

With Jodie hungry as always, and dinner now several

hours away, Shannon decided to make sandwiches as a stopgap. Buttering bread in the kitchen, she tried to work out just how she was going to approach the subject when the time came. If she had saved the tape instead of wiping it she could have played it back to him. That would have been the simplest way. As it was, she could only repeat the message word for word as she so clearly recalled it.

She almost jumped out of her skin when the telephone rang. There were extensions right through the apartment, one of which Kyle had been sitting right beside a few minutes ago. Obviously was still, she realised as the tone ceased only halfway through the second ring.

After only a momentary pause, she carried on buttering bread like an automaton. If the caller was who she believed it to be, matters were going to be brought to a head sooner than planned.

The slight ding on the kitchen extension signifying a replaced receiver elsewhere came after what seemed like hours but was probably less than half a minute. Shannon steeled herself as Kyle came through to the kitchen.

'Did you rewind the tape on the answering machine yesterday?' he asked on an odd note.

'Yes,' she said.

'Why?'

She made herself turn, back against the hard edge of the unit as she met the grey eyes. 'I needed time to take it in.'

Dark brows lifted. 'Take what in exactly?'

'Don't prevaricate,' she said with control. 'It was clear enough. I didn't want to ruin the weekend by bringing it up right away. I'd hoped to discuss it tonight when Jodie was in bed. I should have known she'd ring again, of course.'

Kyle was looking at her with what appeared to be

genuine bafflement. 'Just what the hell are you talking about?'

'Oh, please!' She made a small, impatient gesture. 'At least do me the courtesy of being honest about it! I can hardly pretend it doesn't matter to me, but I'm not going to jeopardise Jodie's future by walking out over it. I can appreciate that you'll feel a commitment where the child is concerned. What I'm *not* prepared to do is share you wholesale with the mother!'

Breathing ragged, she stopped there, searching the clean-cut features for some assurance that he understood what she was saying—unable to fathom the expression in his eyes.

'Don't you have anything to say?' she burst out.

'I think you'd better meet her,' he responded levelly. 'The sooner the better. She's only a few minutes away.'

Shannon stared after him as he left the kitchen, hardly able to believe that he could be so dispassionate about it all. She had no desire to meet the woman. If he had an ounce of real feeling for her, he could surely appreciate that much!

She was still standing there when he returned with the coat she had so recently discarded.

'You'll not need your handbag,' he said. 'We'll be coming back.'

'I'm not coming with you,' Shannon stated flatly, and saw his jaw set.

'Yes, you are. Jodie's gone to bring the lift up.'

'You can't possibly be proposing to take her along too!' she protested.

'We're not leaving her here on her own.' He held out the coat. 'Let's go.'

She gave in because it was better to accompany him of her own free will than be dragged out—as he looked more than capable of doing at the moment—resenting his whole attitude. Anyone would think *she* was the one at fault here!

Jodie had the lift already standing at the floor. She looked from one to the other with lively curiosity, sensing the atmosphere.

'Where are we going now?' she asked as they started the descent.

'To see a friend,' Kyle supplied.

'A very *close* friend,' Shannon couldn't stop herself from tagging on, regretting it instantly. Involving Jodie in this affair at all was bad enough without the innuendo.

Earlier in the day it might have taken just the few minutes he had spoken of to make the journey. At this hour they were into congestion right away. Kyle showed no impatience. There was no gleaning anything at all of what he might be thinking. Jodie's running commentary on anything and everything was a welcome distraction from Shannon's own thoughts.

They reached their destination in an area she wouldn't have considered residential, although there would be flats above the shops and offices, she supposed. Still looking remarkably impassive for a man about to introduce his wife to his mistress, Kyle led the way into a building bearing several brass business plates at the side of the door, none of which Shannon had time to read.

There was a lift, but he chose to take the stairs, mounting to the first floor where a glass door bearing a name Shannon certainly did recognise gave access to a plush reception office. Mind in turmoil, she stood like a dummy as Kyle was greeted with familiarity and not a little pleasure by the young woman leafing through a manuscript at the desk.

'Angela had the champagne on ice all day waiting for you,' she declared. 'We're all thrilled!' She turned the smile on Shannon and the girl at her side. 'You must be too.'

'What about?' asked Jodie with interest when Shannon failed to make any reply.

'Why, the film contract, of course. You don't mean you haven't told them yet?' She switched her attention back to Kyle with a suddenly crestfallen expression. 'Me and my big mouth! I've ruined your surprise.'

'Not in the least,' he returned easily. 'Shannon, Jodie, meet Gerry—short for Geraldine. I assume Angela's in her office?'

'She certainly is. I'll let her know you're on your way through.'

Grey eyes sought green, the sardonicism undiluted. 'You've met my agent before, of course.'

'Once or twice.' Shannon was wishing the ground would open and swallow her up. This was what a suspicious mind combined with an all-too-vivid imagination did for you! She made a small gesture of appeal. 'Kyle, I—'

'Later.' He indicated the short corridor leading off from the reception area. 'This way.'

'Do you want me to wait here?' queried Jodie, drawing a smile Shannon would have given her right arm for at the moment.

'No, you can come and help us celebrate.'

Angela Davis, of Davis and Blackett Enterprises, met them at the door of her office with a welcoming cry.

'Congratulations again, darling! Good to see you too, Shannon! And this must be Jodie. Striking resemblance!' She stepped back, inviting the three of them over the threshold with a sweep of her hand. 'I've left the bottle for you to open. Dom Pérignon, of course!'

'Nothing but the best for D and B clientele,' commented Kyle on a dry note, and she laughed.

'Some, darling, some!'

Shannon watched wryly as the champagne was un-corked and poured, accepting the glass Kyle handed to her without looking at him directly. Mistaken though she'd obviously been in this instance, she still had little faith in him. The earring, for instance. Who was that owned by?

Allowed half a glassful herself, Jodie took an immedi-ate taste, looking totally unimpressed.

'I thought champagne was supposed to be nice,' she complained. 'They drink it all the time in the movies!'

'It's an acquired taste,' Angela told her, amused by the candid appraisal. She raised her glass. 'To box-office success!'

'And now to business,' she added on a brisker note when the toast had been drunk. 'Let's get this deal tied up nice and tight!'

The traffic was heavier than ever when the three of them finally left. By the time they reached the apartment, it was coming up to six-thirty.

'I think we'd be better off staying over, after all,' said Kyle, peeling off his sheepskin jacket. 'We can leave early and drop off the Rover at the house before going into Tonbridge.'

'I don't mind waiting a few more days to start school if we're only going for my uniform,' offered Jodie mag-nanimously.

He grinned. 'We'll manage. How about we ring out for pizzas?'

She grinned back. 'Great!'

'I'll make some coffee while you're doing it,' said Shannon, feeling distinctly *de trop*.

'You haven't said what topping you want,' Jodie pointed out.

'Oh...cheese and tomato, please.' It was the first com-

bination that came to mind, food holding no interest
whatsoever at the moment.

Curling at the edges in the centrally heated atmosphere, the sandwiches made earlier were no appetite
stimulant either. Shannon tipped the lot into the waste
bin and wiped down the work surface before starting on
the coffee. Things couldn't go on like this, she acknowledged ruefully. What mattered was the future, not the
past. If they were to have any kind of marriage at all,
suspicion had to be laid to rest.

Whatever Kyle had on his mind, it made no difference
to his appetite. He and Jodie polished off the whole sub-
stantial order between them, barring the one slice
Shannon managed to force down her throat. They were
so totally at ease with one another, she thought, making
an effort to join in the lively conversation. Nothing must
happen to mar that relationship.

Despatched to bed at nine, Jodie went with only a
token protest. Shannon waited for Kyle to start the ball
rolling with some caustic comment, but she waited in
vain. Hands clasped comfortably behind his head, eyes
closed, he appeared to be listening to the orchestral piece
being played on the radio.

It was she who broke in the end, her voice rough. 'We
have to talk, Kyle.'

'About what?' he asked without opening his eyes.

'You know about what! I'm sorry for jumping to the
wrong conclusion. I should have known you wouldn't
be that careless.'

The firm mouth took on a slant. 'Thanks.'

'I had other reasons for thinking you might be involved with someone,' Shannon went on doggedly.

This time he did open his eyes, expression unreadable.
'Such as?'

When it came to the point, the evidence looked scanty

even to her, but it was too late to retract. 'That telephone call the other morning to start with,' she said. 'It was obviously someone who wasn't expecting to hear a woman's voice. Then there's the earring in your desk drawer.'

'And?' Kyle prompted when she failed to go on.

'That's it,' she admitted reluctantly. 'I realise it doesn't sound a great deal to go on, but—'

'But enough, combined with a lack of trust I'm responsible for in the first place.' The tone was steady. 'I can't say who it was on the phone the other day, although I wouldn't put it past Paula to try making trouble between us again. As to the earring…' he paused, a hint of self-mockery in his smile '…it's there as a memento of the girl I loved and lost.'

Heart thudding, Shannon said huskily, 'Who?'

There was no verbal answer. Scooped out of her chair by strong arms, she was too overcome by emotion to heed the lingering doubts, meeting his lips with abandonment.

Some untold time later she said softly, 'Don't take this the wrong way, but that isn't *my* earring you've got in your desk.'

'Yes, it is.' Kyle brought up a hand to smooth the clinging tendrils of damp hair from her cheek, eyes tender as they roved her captivating face. 'I found it when I was moving your things. You only wore the pair once—when you went to a fancy-dress party as a gypsy fortune-teller. Remember?'

'Hazily,' Shannon confirmed, happy to have that particular doubt despatched. She laughed. 'I think I'd had rather too much to drink that night. I've vague recollections of you sticking me under the shower fully dressed when we got home, to sober me up!' Her brow wrinkled as she sought the memory. 'You were really angry.'

'Furious. I'd caught you kissing our hostess's younger brother in the garden, after flirting with just about every man there!'

Recollections of the actual evening itself were still hazy, but it would have been about that time, Shannon reckoned, when things had started to fall apart. 'I was probably trying to make you jealous,' she said wryly. 'You were losing interest in me. Outside of bed, at any rate.'

Kyle gave a rueful smile. 'Not so much a loss of interest as the realisation that I'd done neither of us any favours in marrying you. You weren't ready for marriage. You needed to be out and about having fun—dancing the night away at discos, doing things I'd got past wanting to do. All the time, at least.'

There was too much truth in what he was saying to be denied. 'I did love you,' she whispered, drawing another smile.

'Infatuation would be closer.'

There was something in that too, Shannon was bound to concede. What she'd felt for him then was not to be compared with what she felt now. She looked long and deep into the grey eyes, still uncertain that what she saw there wasn't a product of wishful thinking.

'Would you have come after me at all if it hadn't been for Jodie?'

Kyle put his lips to the end of her small nose, holding her close. 'When you left I tried convincing myself it was for the best, but it never worked. Jodie simply provided the excuse I needed to come and get you back.'

'If you'd wanted me back that badly, you wouldn't have waited for an excuse,' she said huskily.

'And would you have come back without Jodie as an incentive?'

'I...might have.'

He shook his head. 'No, you wouldn't. You took enough persuading as it was.'

Shannon touched her fingertips to the firm mouth. 'I was terrified of being hurt again. I still am.' She hesitated, reluctant to bring the name up again, yet still needing reassurance. 'Did you ever love Paula?'

'No.' His gaze was direct. 'I didn't sleep with her either.'

The doubt was too deep-seated for immediate eradication. 'If that's true, why didn't you tell me at the time?' she asked huskily.

'I tried to. You wouldn't listen.' His lips twisted. 'I could hardly blame you. I doubt if I'd have been any more prepared to keep an open mind in similar circumstances.'

'But if it wasn't sexual—'

'She offered a ready ear as a friend, that's all—or so I thought at the time. I needed someone to talk to, to advise me where I might be going wrong with you. Who better than another woman?'

'You could have tried my mother.'

There was a sudden humorous glint in his eyes. 'As a matter of fact, it was your mother who thought a baby might settle you down a little. I'd probably have given you another year or so before suggesting it myself, but I took the chance that she might be right.'

Shannon had to smile. 'Trust Mom to come up with something like that. It was always her greatest sorrow that she never managed to have any more babies herself.' She was silent for a moment, studying the handsome features—still not wholly sure of him. 'You must have given Paula *some* reason to think she could have you if she got rid of me for you.'

'No physical reason, I can assure you. I was far too much in love with my beautiful, tempestuous young wife to even think about playing away.' Kyle cupped her face between his hands, his expression softening. 'I still am. Always will be. This past eighteen months has been hell. If you knew how hard I've had to fight to stay away from you!'

'Why did you?' she whispered.

'Because I was trying to do what I thought was best for you. Then this thing with Jodie cropped up, and all I could think of was that now I *had* to get you back. Hearing about Craig was one of the worst moments of my life.'

'I was so unfair to him,' Shannon acknowledged wryly. 'I knew deep down that I'd never love him the way he deserved to be loved. I used him as a buffer against you—against what you made me feel again. I only hope he finds someone who'll really care for him.'

'I imagine they'll be queuing up once it's discovered he's on the market again,' came the dry return, drawing a sudden smile.

'I do believe you're jealous!' she teased.

'You bet I am. I came too darned close to losing you to him.' His voice roughened. 'I love you, Shannon. I *need* you. And not just for Jodie's sake either. I want to spend my life with you, raise a family with you.'

'Even though I can't cook?' she murmured, and saw his mouth curve.

'There's more to life than cooking.'

A whole lot more, she thought blissfully as his lips found hers again.

'He just said my name!' exclaimed Jodie, beaming delightedly at the gurgling occupant of the high chair. 'You're a very clever little boy, Daniel Beaumont!'

'Emulating his big sister,' commented Kyle, buttering

another piece of toast. 'Although two eggheads in one family might be a bit much to handle.'

'We both have perfectly shaped heads, thank you,' came the prompt retort.

Make that three, thought Shannon, looking fondly from husband to daughter to son. It was easy to see who had the strongest genetic line in this household: at six months, Daniel was already the image of his father.

It sometimes seemed more like a few weeks than two years since she and Kyle had got back together again, the time had passed so quickly. Thirty-seven now, he was beginning to show a hint of silver at the temples, but it only served to enhance his masculine appeal. His weight was the same—unlike her own, which still tipped the scales by a few extra pounds. All in the right places, according to Kyle, but men had different ideas of what constituted the ideal feminine figure.

It had been a wonderful two years all round. The adoption had gone through without a hitch, and Jodie had settled down at Silverwood with scarcely a hint of trouble, her talents channelled in the right direction. Kyle was proving really good at being a father, Shannon reflected, feasting her eyes on the handsome profile. Not so dusty as a husband either. And as a lover…

Her pulses went into overdrive at the very memory of the way he'd woken her this morning. Before they'd had time to take precautions, too. Still, she wouldn't be too devastated to find herself pregnant again. Maybe she might even manage to put a little more of *her* stamp on the next one!

'Thought of a new plot, have you?' asked Kyle, jerking her out of it to find him regarding her quizzically. 'You look like a cat faced with a saucer of cream.'

'Just daydreaming,' she said. 'Have you seen the latest box-office figures on *Double Jeopardy*?'

'It seems to be doing pretty well.'

'Stop being so modest. It already beat *Blue Ice*, and that was a big enough hit!'

'Next time you go to Hollywood, can I go too?' asked Jodie.

'Next time he goes to Hollywood, we'll *all* go,' declared Shannon—trusting to luck that she'd be in a suitable condition if and when the time came.

'Do I gather I'm not to be trusted on my own again?' said Kyle with a lift of an eyebrow.

She pulled a face at him. 'Not after seeing that television coverage of the première, with you escorted by two nubile blondes!'

'Not so nubile in close-up,' he returned drily. 'Not so blonde either. It's Land of Illusion in every sense out there, believe me.'

She did believe him. She trusted him too. He might look at other women, he might fancy one on occasion— that was man's nature—but he wouldn't do anything to jeopardise what they had between them because she meant as much to him as he did to her. That she could count on.

'Love you,' she mouthed at him, and saw the grey eyes glint.

'When?' he mouthed back.

'If you two are going to get mushy, I'll take Daniel out for a walk,' said Jodie with an impish grin, picking up on the vibes. 'Come on, little brother—' she lifted the child from the chair '—let's leave the grown-ups to play.'

'One of these days you're going to overstep the mark, young lady,' growled Kyle with mock severity as the pair departed, receiving a chuckle by way of reply.

There was a small silence after the kitchen door closed. Kyle was the first to break it, mouth curving as he surveyed his wife's vibrant face and tumbling golden hair. '*Are* the grown-ups going to play, then?'

'We already did,' Shannon reminded him, tongue-in-cheek. 'Anyway, I've a ton of things to do this morning!'

'Not on a Sunday.' He got to his feet, tightening the belt of his short silk robe with a purposeful gleam in his eyes. 'Obey thy lord and master, wench!'

'Since when did you write historicals?' she scoffed, getting up hastily and backing off as he rounded the table. 'Touch me, and I'll ruin you for life!'

His grin was good to see as always. 'About where I came in—second time around, at any rate. It would have saved a lot of time if I'd done this then...'

Shannon squealed as he swung her up over his shoulder, pummelling at his back with both fists. 'I'll have the law on you, brute!'

'Some risks one just has to take,' he said, making for the door.

Helpless with laughter, Shannon revelled in his muscular strength as he carried her so easily up the stairs. Her very own real-life hero!

HARLEQUIN PRESENTS®

The world's bestselling romance series...
The series that brings you your favorite authors,
month after month:

Helen Bianchin...Emma Darcy
Lynne Graham...Penny Jordan
Miranda Lee...Sandra Morton
Anne Mather...Carole Mortimer
Susan Napier...Michelle Reid

and many more uniquely talented authors!

Wealthy, powerful, gorgeous men...
Women who have feelings just like your own...
The stories you love, set in exotic, glamorous locations...

HARLEQUIN PRESENTS,
Seduction and passion guaranteed!

HPGEN99

Harlequin® Historical

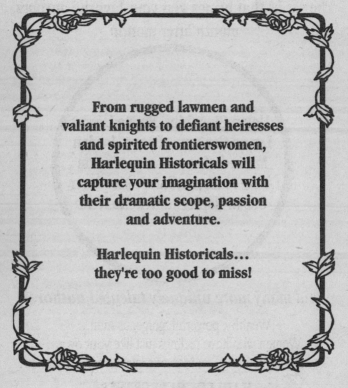

From rugged lawmen and
valiant knights to defiant heiresses
and spirited frontierswomen,
Harlequin Historicals will
capture your imagination with
their dramatic scope, passion
and adventure.

Harlequin Historicals...
they're too good to miss!

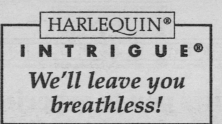

HARLEQUIN SUPERROMANCE®

...there's more to the story!

Superromance. A *big* satisfying read about unforget-
table characters. Each month we offer
four very different stories that range from family
drama to adventure and mystery, from highly emotional stories to romantic comedies—and
much more! Stories about people you'll
believe in and care about. Stories too
compelling to put down....

Our authors are among today's *best* romance writ-
ers. You'll find familiar names and
talented newcomers. Many of them are
award winners—and you'll see why!

If you want the biggest and best
in romance fiction, you'll get it
from Superromance!

Available wherever Harlequin books are sold.

Your Romantic Books—find them at

www.eHarlequin.com

Visit the *Author's Alcove*

➢ Find the most complete information anywhere on your favorite author.

➢ Try your hand in the Writing Round Robin—contribute a chapter to an online book in the making.

Enter the *Reading Room*

➢ Experience an interactive novel—help determine the fate of a story being created now by one of your favorite authors.

➢ Join one of our reading groups and discuss your favorite book.

Drop into *Shop eHarlequin*

➢ Find the latest releases—read an excerpt or write a review for this month's Harlequin top sellers.

➢ Try out our amazing search feature—tell us your favorite theme, setting or time period and we'll find a book that's perfect for you.

All this and more available at

www.eHarlequin.com
on Women.com Networks